"Thank You For Coming To My Rescue,"

Gioia said.

"Forget it. Just don't drive without a spare tire again, all right?"

"No, sir. Yes, sir. I promise, sir."

Thad noticed a gleam of amusement light her eyes. "And don't be such a smartie," he growled with just the threat of a smile on his face. He didn't look directly at her as he let himself out of her home.

"No, sir," Gioia whispered, leaning in her front doorway to watch as he strode out to his muddy dark green car.

Thad got as far as his car and stopped. He decided his mind had already ceased to function halfway across her front porch or he'd never consider doing what he was about to do now. But, damn it, sometimes a man had to act on impulse to avoid getting ulcers!

Or so he told himself as he marched back up to the orange house, up the front steps, across the wooden porch and swept the waiting woman into his arms.

Dear Reader:

Happy New Year! Now that the holiday rush is through you can sit down, kick off your shoes and open the cover of a Silhouette Desire.

As you might know, we'll be continuing the *Man of the Month* program through 1990. In the upcoming year look for men created by some of your favorite authors: Elizabeth Lowell, Annette Broadrick, Diana Palmer, Nancy Martin and Ann Major. Also, we'll be presenting Barbara Boswell's first-Desire-ever as a *Man of the Month*.

But Desire is more than the *Man of the Month*. Each and every book is a wonderful love story in which the emotional and the sensual go hand-in-hand. The book can be humorous or serious, but it will always be satisfying.

So whether you're a first-time reader or a regular, welcome to Desire 1990—I know you're going to be pleased.

Lucia Macro
Senior Editor

DIXIE BROWNING

SHIPS IN THE NIGHT

SILHOUETTE *Desire*

Published by Silhouette Books New York

America's Publisher of Contemporary Romance

SILHOUETTE BOOKS
300 East 42nd St., New York, N.Y. 10017

ISBN: 0-373-05541-2

First Silhouette Books printing January 1990

Books by Dixie Browning

Silhouette Romance

Unreasonable Summer #12
Tumbled Wall #38
Chance Tomorrow #53
Wren of Paradise #73
East of Today #93
Winter Blossom #113
Renegade Player #142
Island on the Hill #164
Logic of the Heart #172
Loving Rescue #191
A Secret Valentine #203
Practical Dreamer #221
Visible Heart #275
Journey to Quiet Waters #292
The Love Thing #305
First Things Last #323
Something for Herself #381
Reluctant Dreamer #460
A Matter of Timing #527

Silhouette Special Edition

Finders Keepers #50
Reach Out to Cherish #110
Just Deserts #181
Time and Tide #205
By Any Other Name #228
The Security Man #314
Belonging #414

Silhouette Desire

Shadow of Yesterday #68
Image of Love #91
The Hawk and the Honey #111
Late Rising Moon #121
Stormwatch #169
The Tender Barbarian #188
Matchmaker's Moon #212
A Bird in Hand #234
In the Palm of Her Hand #264
A Winter Woman #324
There Once Was a Lover #337
Fate Takes a Holiday #403
Along Came Jones #427
Thin Ice #474
Beginner's Luck #517
Ships in the Night #541

Silhouette Christmas Stories 1987

"Henry the Ninth"

For Joe and Jennie
way up there in Kodiak

One

What makes you think I haven't already been invited?"

"Because when you're happy you shout, and if you'd been invited, I'd have heard you bellowing all the way over from Queen Street."

"I never bellow," Gioia said indignantly.

"I'd like to know what you call it."

"Singing?"

"No way," scoffed Edy as she started to efficiently stuff bills into envelopes.

"You wouldn't know singing if you heard it, if that tape you've got in your car is anything to go by."

"If you're referring to my Bruce, I'll have you know he's considered a classic."

"He screams. He doesn't vocalize."

"Oh, but if you ever watched him while he was screaming," Edy said dreamily, "you wouldn't care what he sounded like. Are you going to do it?"

"What, watch your favorite pair of tight jeans bump and grind his way through 'America the Beautiful'? No way."

"You probably hated Elvis, too, didn't you? Honestly, Gioia, sometimes I wonder about you. And, anyway, I wasn't talking about that. I meant T.J. Will you go out with him?"

Gioia rolled up her sleeve to reach down into the aquarium she'd come by to check and stroked her favorite hermit crab. "Actually, I liked his singing okay. I even like some of his old movies, and I know you were talking about T.J., and no thanks." She'd finished all the other plants and aquariums in the office building, leaving Dr. Graham's office till last so that she could visit for a few minutes with her friend.

"Oh, come on, where's your sense of adventure? You're getting stale, Gioia—my husband said T.J. wasn't your type, but I told him that was just because he didn't know you. The guy's a real hunk, honestly. You'd have a ball."

"Thanks, but I think I'll pass, Edy. If he's all that great, he won't have any trouble finding someone else."

"But the dance is just three days off! Who's he going to find in three days? The tickets cost an ear and a kidney."

"Tough, but hardly my problem. Your hunk should have lined up a date before he forked over for the tickets."

Edy sealed the last of the bills to drop off at the post office on her way home. "As it so happens, he had one, smarty. He and Sandy broke up the day after he got the tickets."

"And you expect me to get mixed up in the middle of something like *that*? No thanks. I'm allergic to other women's men."

"Oh, for pity's sake, that's all over. Honestly, Gioia, he's a real doll. And you like music. The band's supposed to be great."

Gioia finished shredding a shrimp and lingered to play with a leggy spider crab. "My book club shipment came today. It looks like a great batch."

"You can read any old time. How often do you get the chance to hear an imported live band and dance with a certified hunk?"

"As opposed to what? A domestic dead one? Come on, Edy, give me a break. The last time I let you talk me into a blind date, I ended up walking three and a half miles in a pair of four-inch heels. The jerk had more hands than a cotton field. So thanks all the same, but I'll pass."

"T.J.'s not like that. He's real sweet, honestly."

"Sweet men are wimps, handsome men are narcissistic, and blind dates give me hives." Gioia checked the temperature in the aquarium and adjusted the cover again. She still had to feed and water Dr. Graham's carnivorous-looking polypody.

"Well, he's definitely no wimp," Edy grumbled as she straightened up the top of her desk. "And he can't help it if he happens to be good-looking, so you can't hold that against him. Gioia, don't pass up this chance just because some creep dumped you a hundred years ago."

"That'll teach me not to discuss my love life with you."

"Ha! What love life? You haven't had a date in months."

"My choice," Gioia said airily. "I've been asked."

She had, too. Twice. Her oil delivery man had offered her an evening to remember—in those exact words—and she'd hastily invented a fiancé who was a U.S. Marine. Then there was the iron-pumping drywall contractor who had invited her to a high school football game to watch his kid brother play. She'd trotted out her fictitious Marine again.

"You're too darn particular. That's your trouble. Wait'll you get a look at T.J. Golden hair, gorgeous tan, great clothes. Plus he's gainfully employed, has charming manners and he drives a brand-new Corvette. Honestly, if I wasn't already married..."

Gioia grabbed her thick braid in one hand and began enumerating her own vital statistics back at Edy. "See this? Ebony. And this?" She pointed to a creamy cheek. "Ivory. These *happen* to be designer jeans I'm wearing—"

"Yeah, that Frenchman—what's his name? Sears de Roebuck."

Ignoring her, Gioia went on. "What's more, I, too, am gainfully employed, I can quote chapter and verse from Miss Manners, and drive a Lincoln Continental."

"Once owned by ol' Abe himself." Edy switched off her desk light. It was almost five-thirty—time to lock up and go home.

"It runs," Gioia insisted.

"All right, then how about this? You both love seafood, you both love music, you both love books—Mack says T.J. reads all the time at work. And Sandy said he's a great dancer."

"Too much in common is worse than not enough. I think bland is the word. Besides, his nose probably comes up to my breastbone." Gioia was five foot ten in her bare feet.

"Gotcha! He's at least six-two," Edy said triumphantly, long earrings jangling as she tossed her mane of blond hair. "Can I tell Mack to tell T.J. you'll go with him? Honestly, Joy—" Edy pleaded, shortening Gioia's already short name "—you won't be sorry. You know you love to dance, and you haven't had a date in ages."

"How crass of you to notice. I've been too busy." That was close to the truth. She had lived in tiny Riverton, North Carolina, across the river from Elizabeth City where all her clients were located, for little over a year. So far, she'd been too busy establishing her various careers and rehabilitating her inheritance to worry about her lack of a social life. The house was coming along. With her plant and aquarium service, her custom baking and the refinishing she did on old paneling and woodwork, she was able to eat, to pay taxes, to send a bit home to help out and even to save something toward her next college term, whenever and wherever that occurred.

Her social life could wait. Elizabeth City's male population wasn't exactly beating a path to her door, and Riverton's total population consisted of one hundred forty-seven souls—none of them eligible males, so far as she knew.

On the other hand, if someone interesting were to turn up, there'd be no stunning, curvaceous younger sister now to distract him. Maybe it was time she tried out her wings again. As long as she kept one foot on the ground, she wouldn't have far to fall.

"All right, you win," she said with a sigh. "I have a feeling I'm going to regret this, but you can tell Mack that if his friend is all *that* desperate, I'll take pity on him. You're sure he's tall enough? I hate feeling like a lighthouse when I go dancing. He does like to dance, doesn't he?"

"*Adores* it! Loves seafood, too, and as for tall, I understand they called him Stretch when he was a kid. Then it's a date?"

"I reckon. And if you make one crack about a two-way stretch, I'll clobber you with this dip net." Gioia's dark blue eyes sparkled with amusement. She dismissed about half of what Edy had told her as pure hype, but the rest should be enough to make it a passable evening. "How fancy is this affair, anyway?"

"Pretty dressy. Got something special?"

"A short navy blue chiffon, but it calls for high heels, so you'd better not be kidding about his height. I've had enough of guys nuzzling my bosom while we're dancing." She found a tube of lotion in her purse and slathered it on, hoping it could perform a miracle on her work-hardened hands before the night of the Yacht Club's big bash.

"You'll be terrific together. I promise you. You finished in here? Mack'll be wondering what happened to me." Edy worked as secretary-receptionist for the doctor whose saltwater aquarium and plants Gioia serviced. Her husband and the paragon who needed a date for the dance both worked at the best men's shop in Elizabeth City— Mack as bookkeeper, his friend T.J. as assistant manager.

T.J. Creed flipped the door sign to read Closed and then returned to the mirror, where he'd been trying on several sport coats that had come in that morning. The brown was great with his hair, but did little to enhance his tan—damn! He'd forgotten to make an appointment for another tanning session and a manicure, and the salon was always busy toward the end of the week. With the dance coming up, it would be packed. His hair could use a good conditioning treatment, too.

He shot his cuff and glanced at his fake Rolex. Thad was running late. The shop closed early on Wednesday, but T.J. had a few errands to run before he got his car out of hock, and he'd just as soon do it on his big brother's expense account. He'd had to wait until today to pick up the Corvette because the cretin in the credit office had refused to give him thirty days—just because he'd been caught short a few times! It was a hell of a note when a gentleman's word meant nothing at all to some jerk with dirty fingernails.

The door rattled, and he slipped off the Harris tweed and hurried to let his older half brother into the shop. "Just let me set the alarm. Man, you sure took your time getting here."

Thad leaned against the door, flipped the keys to his dark green Ford into the air and caught them. He'd gotten into town late the night before, and he'd been out all morning scouting the territory. It had been nearly two years since the two men had last seen each other, and he looked now for some new sign of maturity. T.J. had always been a charming scoundrel—a bit too handsome for his own good, yet still somehow likable.

Sometimes Thad wondered why he bothered. All they had in common was a father who had always been far more interested in promoting his career and collecting rich young wives than in parenting. Still, he'd tried to keep in touch, and when the case he was working on had brought him to the area where T.J. was now living, he'd decided that a fraternal visit would make an excellent excuse to hang around.

Or the case would make an excellent excuse to see the only relative he gave half a damn about—he wasn't sure which.

"Let's get out of here," T.J. said. "Mack got me a date for the Yacht Club dance, and I've gotta get my car out of hock."

"Whatever happened to Sandy what's her name?" Thad asked when they reached his car.

The younger man flashed his brother one of the smiles that had cut a wide swath through the female population of Pasquotank County. "She had marriage on the brain, man. I ask you, do I look like husband material to you?"

Thad grinned and slid under the wheel of his three-year-old sedan. The question was purely rhetorical. They both knew—Thad from personal experience and T.J. from observation—that the Creed men were rotten risks when it came to marriage. At least his kid brother was considerate enough to save some poor woman from undergoing a miserable experience.

"Head for the bridge," T.J. said. "I want to run over to Riverton and check out my new lady's address before I pick her up. Gotta be sure I can find it in the dark, right?"

"What about your car?"

"We'll get it later. They're open till five."

Thad took the bridge that linked Pasquotank and Camden Counties. He knew his way around, having pored over navigational charts and checked out, on foot or by car, every creek big enough to hide a rowboat. Riverton was even smaller than nearby Elizabeth City. Most of its residents were retired; the rest either farmed or worked in Norfolk or Elizabeth City. Counting both sides of the river, there were half a dozen commercial marinas and several times that number of private docks and boat houses, most of which could easily absorb a stolen boat until it could be safely turned over to a new owner.

Riverton, with its modest yachting community, looked like the better prospect. And the ketch Thad had followed up from Florida, originally named the *Belle Star* and renamed the *Starfish*, was somewhere close by. Thad could feel it in his bones.

"Turn right at the post office onto Queen and keep going," T.J. instructed.

Ten minutes later Thad asked, "How far on Queen? We're running out of houses."

"Look for Murphy on the mailbox. It's number twenty-seven, I think."

"Somehow I can't see you with a blind date. What happened to your little black book?"

"The top of the line is already snapped up for the dance. I don't fool around with seconds."

Thad gave him a cutting look. "I don't even want to know how you classify your women, but aren't you taking a risk? What if she doesn't, uh, come up to your standards?"

"Mack knows my taste in women. He said she owns her own home and business and looks like a fashion model. I can settle for that in an emergency."

"Murphy coming up on the right," Thad said, slowing down as they neared a narrow two-story frame house, which was in the process of being painted a brilliant shade of orange. Surrounded by harvested cornfields and backed by a somber pine forest, it was startling, to say the least. "Must be some mistake," he muttered. "Did your friend mention an orange house?"

"Nope. He just said her name was Joy and that she was supposed to be a real looker—tall, blue eyes, long black hair. Friend of his wife. She's got some kind of business that takes her around to lots of doctors' offices. Some kind of decorator, maybe. Anyhow, that's how Mack's wife met her." He rolled down his window, and both men were immediately assaulted by the sound of a cassette player turned up full blast. It was perched on one end of the scaffold, and from the sound that emerged from the twin speakers, all the hounds of hell had been let loose. The painter, who was seated in the middle of the plank, rhythmically slapped on paint in time with the beat. She appeared to be howling along with the music.

"Want to stop and ask her if this is the right place, just to be sure?" Thad suggested.

"You gotta be kidding. Don't you notice anything?"

"Orange house? A recording of fire sirens? What's to notice?"

"Mack said she was tall, right? That one's got to be six feet if she's an inch. Long black hair, right? That's no yellow ponytail dangling down to her fanny. It's the only house in sight, and you saw the name on the mailbox. Man, I've been had. Let's get out of here."

"Come on. Give her a chance. Besides, how many women paint their own houses? She's probably just a contractor."

"You see any sign of a contractor's van?"

"Now that you mention it, no."

"You call yourself a P.I.? You couldn't find your—"

"Okay, okay, I get the picture. Look, she's probably not so bad. I mean, that's a pretty spunky thing to do—paint a house."

"I'm not interested in spunky. I want a woman who looks good, smells good and who's good in bed, not one who can beat me at arm wrestling. Let's get out of here, okay?"

Thad took one last look at the woman on the scaffolding. He had to admit that she didn't look much like the type of woman T.J. usually went out with. On the other hand, T.J. had already invited her to the dance.

Of course, Thad reminded himself, he wasn't his brother's keeper, let alone the keeper of his brother's women. The two of them disagreed on almost every topic but one: neither of them was interested in marriage. T.J., because he'd seen the results of his father's lamentable record—three wives, and God knows how many mistresses. Thad, because he'd grown up with his mother's bitterness and had heard too many times the story of how she'd put her husband through school only to be discarded like yesterday's garbage when he was ready to reap the rewards of his expensive education.

Thad had grown up trying to be as unlike his father as he knew how, and in that, at least, he'd succeeded. But when he'd met Jackie Rettiger he'd forgotten a whole lifetime of lessons. He'd lost his head, his heart, and damn near everything else, including his life, before it had finally sunk in. On anything but a temporary basis men and women together were strictly poison.

"Orange. Can you beat it?" T.J. shook his head and rolled up his window. His mind was obviously made up.

"It'd serve you right if she used the leftover paint from her house and touched up your damn car. You're a real jerk, boy. You know that?"

"Hey, don't bug me, okay? We can't all be saints. So I got all the looks and charm in the family and you got all the character. I can live with that."

Thad had to grin. "One of these days you're going to meet a woman who'll leave her footprints right down the middle of your artificially tanned backside."

"Sounds interesting. Come on, let's go get my car out of the hands of those damn pirates. I've gotta scout up another date for this weekend, and I need all the help I can get."

Thad picked up speed and eventually found a place to turn around in the driveway of a sprawling and rather dilapidated old farmhouse a quarter of a mile down the road. He headed back toward town, but slowed unconsciously to get a last look at the long-legged house painter as he passed by the orange house again. A broad-brimmed straw hat was perched squarely on top of her head, and between the ragged end of a pair of paint-stained jeans and an equally paint-stained pair of high-topped sneakers that were primarily green, there was a length of ankle that looked . . . promising.

Thad had a sudden desire to know what she looked like from the front. Regardless of what she looked like, though, she had to have a sense of humor. Any woman who would paint a house orange . . .

What the hell, he thought. It was none of his business. "So what are you going to tell her?" he asked T.J. finally.

"Nothing."

"Come on. You can't just not show up."

"Okay, so I'll send her some roses and a note. I had to go out of town unexpectedly. Family illness. Satisfied?"

"No, but it's better than nothing. You're really a sweet guy. All heart." Thad downshifted with unnecessary force and took the corner a little too fast. It wasn't like him to drive recklessly. Hell, it wasn't like him to be curious about some strange woman's backside.

Or rather, her front side. He'd seen her backside—patched jeans, high-topped sneakers, rope belt and all.

"Look, you gotta understand," T.J. said earnestly. "I've got a reputation to maintain, and anyway, what's the big deal? Nobody takes blind dates seriously. Now get a move on. I want to pick up my car and see if I can scalp these tickets. I only bought 'em because Sandy wanted to go to the dance, and I'm practically flat broke."

Thad dropped T.J. off at the auto repair shop, dismissing the situation from his mind. He had enough troubles of his own without borrowing more. His kid brother hadn't changed. The poor woman was lucky, whether she knew it or not. If she'd gone out with him, she might have had the poor taste to fall for that skin-deep charm of his, and then a lot more than her pride would have ended up getting hurt when he dumped her, as he inevitably would. In that way he was too much like their father.

As it was, she'd escape with a dozen roses and a nicely worded lie, and in a few days she'd forget all about it.

Thad found his way to T.J.'s Riverside Drive address. Actually, it was a studio apartment that had been built over an unused boat house. Damp and drafty, it was still undeniably attractive. And at the moment it offered a bit of much-needed privacy. T.J. had told him he'd be out for a while, test-driving his car and looking for someone to buy his tickets. That meant there would be plenty of time to scramble a couple of eggs, catch the news, work on his notes and check with his office back in Raleigh.

It was beginning to look as if he'd have to rent a boat. He hated Dramamine duty! He'd tracked the *Belle Star* all the way up from Fort Lauderdale without having to take to the water, and he'd just as soon keep it that way.

Thad poured over his notes, making frequent references to one or another of the navigational charts that littered T.J.'s breakfast bar. The thing that made it rough was that by the time she'd even cleared her home port, she'd been sporting a new set of sails and probably her new name. Con Summerfield had owned her for less than three months, most of them spent in nonstop partying from what Thad had been able to determine. But sober, even Summerfield would have had trouble recognizing her now unless he happened to have an unusually keen eye for the line of a boat.

Thad's eye was strictly an acquired one. By the time he'd taken on his second stolen-yacht case, he had put in enough hours on the subject of boats to have been able to build one—if not to sail it. By now he knew every teak plank and bronze screw in the quarter of a million dollar hull. He should be able to identify the *Belle Star* in spite of all the superficial changes she'd undergone, once he found her.

But finding her was only the first step. Boarding her with enough time and privacy for a stem-to-stern search would be the real test. He had flown down to Palm Beach at Summerfield's request—the only place to start on a case like this was at the beginning. The moment he'd learned from a contact in Fort Lauderdale that she was sporting a different set of sails, he'd sent his best legman out to locate the originals. If his man could find those, with the original ID numbers, possibly a receipt, it would be enough to get a search warrant. Maybe. On the other hand, if the originals were still on board, and he could find them, it should take less than five minutes to pin down her identity as Summerfield's stolen yacht.

But first he had to find her. Then he had to get himself on board for five minutes. After that he'd start praying that the damn pirate had overlooked a few HINs. The dumber ones didn't even realize there was such a thing as a hidden identification number on most yachts until they'd been nailed to the mast by a small string of numerals tucked away in an insignificant place.

But this guy was no amateur. After nearly a month Thad had come to know him quite well, and the more he learned about his quarry the less he liked him. It was no longer a game of hide-and-seek.

Thad checked in with his answering service, then called his secretary at home for a status report on the other cases his agency was handling. There were only three. It wasn't a big outfit.

He polished off four scrambled eggs, several slices of raisin toast and a pint of coffee. T.J. still hadn't come home by the time he fell asleep over the editorial pages of the *News and Observer*.

* * *

Gioia hung her navy blue chiffon on a hangar on the back stoop to air out any remaining trace of mothballs. She switched on *Afternoon at the Metropolitan* in time to hear the end of an overture, then got out the ingredients for the two pecan pies she had to deliver at six. It would be cutting it close, but she'd already shampooed her hair, which took even longer to blow-dry than it did to air-dry. Her fingernails were a mess as usual. She hadn't been able to get all the paint off and made a mental note to put on a couple of coats of polish while the pies were baking. If she went all out on the makeup, maybe no one would notice a few calluses and the occasional orange paint spatter. She hated to go out reeking of eau de turpentine.

Beating egg yolks, she hummed along with the familiar aria, now and then clutching the eggbeater to her distinctly undivalike bosom. Eight months of voice lessons had been more than enough to tell her that it had been a fluke that she'd been vocalizing before she could even talk. As much as she loved music, she had *not* been born to sing.

The phone rang just as she slid the pies into the oven, and she hurried to answer it. It was about time this wonder boy of Edy's called her to let her know when he'd be picking her up. He might have all the time in the world, but she was running on a tight schedule.

"You haven't chickened out, have you?" demanded a familiar voice.

"Oh, Edy. I gave my word, fool that I am. You realize I won't know a soul there, don't you? I only hope the food and the music are worth it."

"Don't worry. T.J. knows everybody. He'll introduce you around. What time is he picking you up?"

"I've no idea. So far I haven't heard a word from him. Maybe he's changed his mind."

"No way. He probably figures everyone knows when the thing starts. Half the people in town will be there. Mack and I would, too, if I hadn't promised to keep Mack's sister's kids this weekend. Lousy timing, huh?"

"Couldn't you subcontract the job just for tonight?"

"With those monsters? Honey, they've been blacklisted by every baby-sitter in this part of the country."

"I hope you're getting well paid."

"Peggy's keeping all four dogs while we go to Cozumel the first week in December. Look, I called to ask if you'd like to borrow my fur. It's supposed to turn cold before morning."

"I plan to be snug in bed by morning. Alone. Anyway, I've got a white angora shawl, and if the band's good, I won't get chilly. It's been so long since I've danced with a nice, tall man...."

It had been a long time since she'd danced with anyone, Gioia mused later as she squinted into the bathroom mirror to see if her mascara had smeared. She'd gone all out for the occasion, puffing her hair out to hide the unfortunate Murphy ears and gathering it on top of her head with a pair of rhinestone combs.

Despite all her precautions, her hair would still probably come tumbling down the first time she got out on the dance floor. It was as straight as a poker and much too heavy, and she would have had it cut years before if not for her neck, which she felt was rather more like a giraffe's than a swan's.

She slipped into her evening shoes and took a few experimental steps across the room. It had been ages since she'd had occasion to wear them. As dearly as she loved to dress up, when one was pushing six feet, one didn't look one's best in ruffles and high heels.

She switched on the porch light, locked the front door and settled herself on the swing to wait. It was seven-thirty, and according to Edy, the dance started at eight. In case her date had trouble finding her house, she needed to be ready to wave him in. Edy had said he drove a white Corvette, and there weren't that many white Corvettes cruising along Queen Street. Most of the traffic out this far consisted of pickup trucks and the occasional farm tractor traveling from field to field.

"The hell you didn't!" Thad roared.

"Oh, come on, don't make such a big deal of it. She's probably not expecting me anyway. You know how these blind dates are—one or the other always gets cold feet."

"Damn it, T.J., you always were a selfish jerk! You asked the woman out. You owe her something! What happened to the roses and the excuse you were going to send?"

The younger man flushed, which only enhanced his golden good looks. "The florist is a real dork."

"In other words, you're in hock up to your Adam's apple as usual. You sold the tickets, didn't you? What the hell did you do with the money?"

"A guy has to keep up appearances."

"It's still not too late," Thad said. "You could take her out to that supper club you were telling me about. She's probably a lot of fun. Your friend wouldn't give you a bum steer about a thing like that. She's probably a real doll."

"Look, quit bugging me, will you? Gigi's picking me up in about five minutes. We'll be at her cottage at Kitty Hawk if you need to reach me. I'll be back in time to go to work Monday."

"Gigi, huh? With a cottage at Kitty Hawk. Boy, you've got it made, haven't you? One of these days I hope some woman mops the deck with your face."

At the sound of a car horn out on the street, T.J. shrugged, scooped up his crocodile overnight bag and tendered a mock salute. "So call her yourself. Tell her I broke my leg or something if it'll make you sleep any better."

Thad's suggestion was both prompt and extremely crude.

Twenty minutes later he turned off on Riverton Road and headed for Queen Street. He'd changed into the all-purpose suit he carried with him in case of emergencies, having learned the hard way to be prepared for any eventuality when he was on a job. He'd once lost a guy he'd been tailing when he'd been stopped at the door of some uptown club.

What was he going to tell her—the truth, or some lie to spare her feelings? He should have called. It would have been a hell of a lot easier.

All right, so he was a coward. All his life he seemed to have been trying to make up for shortcomings, real or imagined, in his heritage. He'd like to think that T.J.'s lack of responsibility came from his mother's side of the family, but it was Thaddeus Senior all over again. Their mutual father had divorced Thad's mother, who had helped put him through medical school. He had then coldly chosen his field not out of any real interest, but because plastic surgery was lucrative and rarely demanded night calls. He'd gone on to marry two wealthy and much younger women in succession, divorcing them both when they'd begun to cramp his flamboyant style.

So, someone in the Creed family owed this Murphy woman an apology, Thad told himself. It looked as if he'd been elected. He would simply explain very briefly that something had come up and that T.J. had been called out of town, and—

God, there she was, waiting for him! All dressed up like a doll in a toy-store window.

Thad cleared his throat and straightened his tie. This wasn't going to be quite as easy as he'd hoped. He'd planned to ring the doorbell, speak his piece and get the hell out. Now he was going to have to walk up that long, narrow path, climb the gray wooden steps and stand there in front of her, lying his fool head off. If there was one thing Thad had never been good at—and, actually, there were quite a few—it was lying.

"All right," he muttered under his breath as he straightened his black tie again, "here we go, for better or worse. Five minutes from now it'll be all over and you can go somewhere quiet and have a beer."

Two

Gioia watched the car slow down as it approached her house. If that was a white Corvette, she'd been inhaling too many varnish fumes. Probably looking for JoElla Haley's place half a mile farther on. JoElla did a lot of heavy-duty sewing for boat owners.

The dark green Ford stopped at the end of her driveway. A man got out. Head down, hands rammed into the pockets of a dark suit, he sauntered up her front walk. One thing was obvious: he wasn't her date. She couldn't tell about his taste in food, books or music, but he was neither tall nor handsome enough to fit the description.

A tremor walked down her spine. Not exactly fear— more like excitement. Not that there was anything exciting about a scowling, tough-looking stranger with enormous shoulder pads.

On closer inspection, though, she decided the shoulders weren't padded. Off-the-rack suits, which his obviously was, simply weren't made to accommodate muscle-bound jocks, which he obviously was.

"You must be looking for Mrs. Haley," she said by way of greeting. Even at its firmest her voice had the same huskiness that had hinted early on that God had never intended her to be the next great mezzo-soprano.

"Um, Miss Murphy? Miss Joy Murphy?"

He sounded almost shy, if a man built like a compact armored car could be shy. Actually, he wasn't all that bad-looking, either. Not exactly what one would call handsome, but there was something rather appealing about him just the same.

She drew her stole closer about her shoulders. "Actually, it's Gioia." From habit she spelled it out. "My father's idea. It was his mother's name. And as if that wasn't enough, he followed it up with Angelica, Octavius, Trevor, Rutherford, Chloe, Desdemona and Anastasia. Are you aware of the possible nicknames for a kid named Anastasia?"

"Uh, Anna? Stacy?"

At least he was no longer scowling. In fact, he looked slightly dazed. "Try Nasty," she said with a low chuckle.

"You mean you have, ah—" his fingers moved rapidly against his thigh "—nine names?"

"Good memory. No, I got off with the usual number. The rest are siblings. Sorry. You can't possibly be interested in the Murphy roll call. If you're looking for Mrs. Haley, she lives about a half mile farther along the road, just after the sharp turn."

"The...no, I was looking for a Joy, I mean, a Gioia Murphy. It's about the dance at the—"

"You're T. J. Creed?" Trying not to sound too amazed, Gloria vowed to wash her friend's mouth out with soap at the first opportunity.

"Thaddeus Creed," he said. Before he could continue, though, her conscience jerked her up by the scruff of the neck. She slid over on the swing and swept her skirt aside. "Please, won't you have a seat? Not on the chair. I painted it and it's still sticky."

He sat, and didn't look so short. Actually, he wasn't. It was his wedge-shaped build, wide shoulders and narrow hips that made him look stocky.

But he certainly wasn't six feet two, either!

Gioia thought about what she'd told Edy about short men nuzzling her bosom while they danced, and an image rose in her mind. She looked at him out of the corner of her eye and felt herself grow warm. That darn imagination of hers was getting out of hand!

It was hunger. She should have eaten something. Hunger always affected her brain. All right, so Edy had stretched the truth a little. Height wasn't everything. And blond hair usually got darker in the winter months. Unlike her sister, Angelica, T.J., or Thaddeus—whatever he called himself—probably wasn't vain enough to bother touching his hair up, and that was okay, too. Gioia had never cared much for vain men.

But handsome?

With only the smallest of sighs she took stock of her date. His thick brown hair needed a trim. The sideburns were lighter—gray, she suspected—which should have made him look distinguished but didn't. His face could be called rugged if one were kind. Stubborn, if one were perceptive. Bulldoggy would be an apt description, she decided, remembering a favorite family pet. Bear had been a bowlegged, sad-eyed mixture of boxer and English bull—stubborn and ferocious-looking, but, oh, so sweet.

The smile she gave him was more in fond memory of Bear, but he couldn't know that. "Well, I'm delighted to meet you, T.—that is, Thaddeus.'' She held out a hand, and after a slight hesitation he took it. Her hands were hard, but his were like iron. Warm, dry and electrifying. He didn't release it right away, almost as if he didn't quite know what it was doing here. And then he dropped it, cleared his throat and stared at an upended rocker.

Shy, she thought. Edy couldn't have been more wrong. And Gioia couldn't have been happier. He was no movie star, but then if he were, he wouldn't have needed a blind date. She was a lot more comfortable with this type of man—at least she would be once he got over his shyness, and once she got over this peculiar reaction. It was a little being tickled all over with the tip of a very soft feather. Disconcerting, but not at all unpleasant.

''Well...shall we be on our way?'' she finally asked. ''I hate to tell you how long it's been since the last time I danced, but I promise I'll be gentle with you. I hope it's like riding a bicycle.''

''About the dance, Miss Murphy...''

''Gioia. Or Joy, if you'd rather.''

''Gioia. It's, uh, a real nice name. But about the dance. I just came by to tell you that, well, you see, the tickets...''

He couldn't afford the tickets, she thought. Edy had said they were expensive, but she'd also said he'd already bought them, hadn't she? ''The tickets?'' she prompted when he seemed to be having trouble with his collar. His neck was as muscular as the rest of him—he'd probably be a lot more comfortable in jeans and a sweatshirt.

''Yeah, well, there was this guy who really needed another pair at the last minute and, uh, I'd heard the band was pretty bad....'' Thad closed his mind to the utter stupidity of what he was about to do. ''And, well, anyway, I thought if it was all the same to you, we'd drive across the river to this supper club." Pray God he could get reservations. He'd make some excuse to stop at a service station and call ahead.

Gioia blinked, and Thad wondered if her eyelashes ever got tangled up. They were sure as hell long enough, and curly, too.

"Oh, well, sure," she said. "That's just fine. I mean, they never have much in the way of food at these Yacht Club affairs, do they? I spent the whole afternoon baking pies and didn't have time to eat a bite."

Thad didn't know what kind of food, if any, they served at the local dances. He didn't particularly care. More to the point, he didn't know how the hell he'd ended up inviting her out to dinner. All he knew was that he'd taken one look at that face—the flaring cheekbones, the big, tilted eyes that were so dark he couldn't even see the color, the square little jaw and the glistening red lips that seemed designed for laughing, plus a few even more interesting things—and he'd felt this awful sinking sensation in the pit of his belly.

She's the one, man.

The hell you say!

Call me a liar, but don't say I didn't warn you.

Thad shrugged off the sudden attack of nerves. He'd been working too hard without a break. He deserved a few hours off—dinner, a pretty women to look at to take his mind off all the time he'd spent slogging through wetlands and paddling leaky skiffs in the dead of night just to get a quick look into a lot of stinking boat houses.

Besides, what harm could it do? He was pretty sure she thought he was T.J. There was no point in telling her any differently, since he wouldn't be seeing her again. At least that would save him from having to lie for the jerk.

Forty-five minutes later Thad watched his brother's blind date tuck into a seafood platter that would have fed a family of four. There had been no trouble getting reservations, because half the population of two counties was at the club dance.

"This broiled bluefish is outstanding! I don't know why on earth you ordered beef," Gioia said as she speared another scallop that had been sautéed to a turn. "Mmm, marvelous! Want one?"

"No thanks. I'm, ah, allergic to seafood."

"Allergic? But I thought . . ."

Her eyes widened in surprise, and he was struck again by their startling beauty. Even without those remarkable lashes, her eyes were huge, and tilted in a way that gave her a look of laughter even when her face was in repose, which, between talking and eating, it seldom was.

But it was the color of her eyes that Thad found most remarkable. They were so damn blue! All right, so most eyes that weren't brown or gray or green were probably blue. Hers were different. They were *blue* blue, like the light on top of his cruiser when he'd still been on the force—that kind of traffic-stopping, adrenaline-pumping blue.

"What?" he asked, belatedly realizing she was waiting for the answer to a question he seemed to have missed.

"I said, do you come from a large family, too?"

"Oh, no. One half brother, that's all."

Gioia decided on the spot to shift the conversation to a safer topic. A half sibling could mean he'd come from a broken home, and she didn't want to touch on any tender places—at least not on their first date.

It didn't occur to her that she was taking for granted there'd be a second one. "What sort of work do you do, Thaddeus? I seem to remember hearing that you worked with Mack at the Gentleman's Place."

"No, that's my—ah, half brother," he said, pretending not to notice her look of confusion. "I'm in business for myself now. How about you? What sort of work do you do?" Sooner or later he was going to have to ask about that god-awful orange house of hers. Tactfully, of course.

Her lips were glistening with melted butter, and Thad had a hard time pulling his gaze away. He'd never realized before what an aphrodisiac melted butter could be.

"You name it, I've probably done it," she replied. "Currently I'm taking care of three saltwater aquariums—I think that's supposed to be aquaria, but it sounds sort of pretentious, doesn't it? And plants. I look after the ones at the mall, and in several office buildings, and I do custom baking. Birthday cakes, wedding cakes, a few special pies—you know."

They discussed the fact that all the pastries advertised as homemade usually weren't, then went on to talk about the lack of industry in the northeast corner of North Carolina. Thad toyed with his beef while Gioia polished off her last french fry and began nibbling on her parsley garnish.

Her teeth were as white as snow. Not too large, not too small—and not quite perfect, which appealed to him enormously for reasons he was at a loss to explain.

What the devil had he been thinking of, to get involved with one of T.J.'s victims? If there was one thing he'd learned early, it was to steer clear of soft, disarming women. Someone always got hurt. And while it damn well wasn't going to be him, he didn't want it to be her, either.

Okay, so he'd show her a good time, feed her as much as she'd eat and then take her home. But the next time, that jackass brother of his could haul his own bacon out of the fire!

Thad's scowl deepened as he caught the scent of her unique wildflower perfume over the smell of grilled steak and mixed seafood. He shifted uncomfortably on the gray velvet chair, dropped his napkin and leaned over to retrieve it, accidentally subjecting himself to a glimpse of a pair of long legs clad in a film of something sheer, dark and unbelievably sexy. She'd slipped off her shoes, and her right foot covered over her left, giving her a pigeon-toed look that was awkward and touching—and totally sexy.

Suddenly he was acutely, uncomfortably, embarrassingly, aroused. Thank God for long tablecloths! He sat up and tugged at his collar. "Uh, so...you bake cakes and look after fish and plants. That's, uh, an unusual way to make a living, isn't it?" Was it hot in here, he thought, or was it just him?

T.J.'s source had been correct about one thing: she could have made it as a model easily. She had what it took. He couldn't honestly say he'd never met a more beautiful woman, but he'd never met one who could turn him on so fast. All she'd done was eat, talk and take off her shoes. God help him if he ever got his arms around her, which he knew with sinking certainty, he was going to try to do even if it killed him.

"Did I tell you I'm also a painter," she asked. "Not the artistic type, but the other kind."

"Hmm. Oh, yeah, I noticed the scaffolding on your house."

"Oh, that. Actually, I specialize in restoring and refinishing old paneling and woodwork, but my house was in such bad shape that when one of the boys at the paint store messed up a batch of exterior and they offered to let me have it at cost, I couldn't resist."

"You're painting over the orange, then?"

"No, over the white—or what used to be white. How do you like it?"

"Oh, it's, ah, colorful, isn't it?" he said bravely.

"It was supposed to be something called Edenton Gold, but the boy added a whole tube instead of half a tube of red, and there was no way of getting it out. I thought about mixing in a tube of green to make it brown, but it would've been a muddy brown, sort of dark caramel. Chocolate on a house is okay, but caramel is . . ."

She shook her head, and Thad watched, fascinated, as an intricate twist of hair began to slither down the side of her head. Luckily her ear stopped it before it got too far.

"Anyway," she continued, "I thought I'd do some planting once I get the painting finished. I figure barn red for the trim, which will make the orange look more yellow, and then if I plant a few pyracanthas and some vines. Polygonum grows fast and it'll cover a lot of territory. Then maybe a few viburnum for the berries. What do you think?"

Thad didn't know what to think by that time. In between turning orange into brown and planting things that sounded suspiciously carnivorous, she'd managed to put away an astonishing amount of food for someone whose waist looked fragile enough to snap at a touch.

Along with being aroused, he was now also dangerously bemused. And Thaddeus wasn't accustomed to having his mind meddled with. It made him uncomfortable. It even made him a little angry.

"If you're through, shall we go?" he suggested curtly.

She looked surprised. And then she looked wistfully toward the bandstand, where a barely adequate combo was struggling with something that vaguely resembled "Moon River."

"Oh, I thought we, that is, I hoped . . ."

"Dessert?" A little desperately he summoned the waiter, asked for a dessert menu, then had it recited to him instead.

"The lemon pie—is it topped with meringue, whipped cream or plastic foam?" Gioia inquired politely.

"Ma'am," the waiter said, "I dunno, but it sure don't look like my ma's. You'd be better off with the peach cobbler, and I could bring you a pitcher of cream."

Thad sipped his third cup of black coffee while Gioia put away a generous serving of cobbler. The waiter hovered anxiously until she pronounced it delicious. Then he smiled as if it were a great personal relief to him.

Black coffee always ate holes in his gut this time of night. Too much acid. "About done? Good. Looks like we might miss the traffic."

The traffic? Gioia thought. What traffic? Even on a Saturday night there wasn't enough traffic between Elizabeth City and Riverton to scare the crows off the highway.

The band was tackling another old Andy Williams standby, but with slightly better results. "You wouldn't care to help me work off a few of those calories, would you?" she asked wistfully. Darn it, she'd been promised a dance, and she'd set her hopes on it. Thad's eyes, which were rather nice—warm, hazel and slightly wary at the moment—widened perceptively.

"You mean—?"

"I mean, dance, of course. What'd you think I wanted to do, walk home? Not in these shoes, I assure you."

He sighed, looked around rather frantically for the waiter and then turned back to her. Even to get his arms around her, he couldn't risk it. "I don't dance much these days," he declared. "Sorry."

That did it. Her fabulous date, who was supposed to be tall, blond and handsome, who loved seafood and dancing and books and good music, and all the things she adored, had turned out to be—well, hardly tall, blond and handsome, at least. And he was allergic to seafood and didn't dance. Great!

She tried again. "I understand you're a music fan. Did you hear *Il Trovatore* this afternoon? I had to miss the second act when I ran out of corn syrup and had to dash out to the market."

For Thad that was the last straw. He grabbed the check and stood, muttering something about an early night. He had to get rid of her, and quick. She wasn't his type at all.

At the same time, she was altogether too *much* his type! It had been years since he'd had trouble controlling his libido, but after a couple of hours in the company of this long-stemmed beauty, with her guileless face and her sexy body, he was about to set off the sprinkler system!

It was T.J.'s fault. He'd kill him. He'd hang around until Monday morning just for the chance of rearranging those pretty features of his, and then he'd find himself a motel somewhere on the waterway and wind up this damn case, one way or another!

Gioia was silent during the ride home. It had evidently rained a bit while they'd been inside, and the pavement gleamed softly under the streetlights as they passed through Riverton's two-block business district and headed out Queen Street.

As dates went, it had been pretty dismal. She'd felt like offering to pay for her dinner, but one look at Thad's face had told her the offer wouldn't have been appreciated.

All in all, she'd had a rotten time, and she couldn't help but think he'd been even more miserable, which led her to wonder what Mack had told him about *her*. How had he described her? Tall, skinny, dark hair, big ears, jaw too square and nose too short, but not bad with a good paint job?

Maybe he'd mentioned her baking. Thad had mentioned during dinner how long it had been since he'd had any home cooking. Feeling she had to do something to end the evening on a positive note, she turned to him. "Look, I baked an extra pie today, if you'd care to come in for dessert. You didn't have any."

They pulled up in front of her house, and she noticed he didn't switch off the engine. And by the way, Edy, she asked silently, whatever happened to that white Corvette you promised me? Not that she had anything against dusty green Fords, but it was just one more score she had to settle with her friend.

"No thanks," Thad told her after a moment. "I've got a few calls to make. Business, that is. But thanks."

He was out of the car and at her door before she could get her feet back into her shoes, but he'd still left the engine running. So much for sweet and shy and tough and sexy, she thought with a tired sigh. This time she couldn't blame it on Angie. She'd managed to lose this one with no help from her sister.

The mall's schefflera needed attention—all forty-seven of them—and someone had carved their initials in the trunk of Dr. Graham's dracaena, eliciting a panicky call from Edy. The Taylors' aquarium had picked up a parasite, thanks to their habit of accepting specimens from dubious sources, including, Gioia feared, leftover bait minnows.

She had decided to say nothing at all to Edy about her date. Let her wonder. Let her stew in her own juice. It wasn't entirely by accident that she'd chosen to do Dr. Graham's office at the busiest time of day. The waiting room was full, the phone was ringing off the hook and Edy was having trouble convincing a determined woman that the doctor really couldn't work her in today, in spite of the unattractive rash on her ring finger.

Edy gave her a questioning look, which Gioia answered with a big grin and a thumbs-up sign. If Edy had a shred of conscience, that should make her squirm.

She wouldn't get away with it forever, but by Wednesday, when she made her rounds again, perhaps Edy would have forgotten.

Gioia's schedule allowed three visits a week to her aquariums. But if the owners were out of town, she went twice daily for feeding and lights. In between, the owners were instructed concerning how much and how often to feed and what danger signals to look out for.

She did plants and aquariums together when a client had both, but the mall was her biggest customer, as well as her biggest headache. It was small, as malls went, but still large enough for its planters to collect an amazing assortment of debris. She'd fished out tons of trash from under the luxuriant foliage—ballpoint pens, disposable diapers, plastic combs, toys, a torn photograph, several pieces of cutlery from the restaurant, more than a few moneyless billfolds, and once even a gun, which had necessitated a visit from the police.

That had terrified her so much that for days she'd been afraid to lift a leaf!

By Friday she'd all but forgotten her disastrous date with T. J. Creed, except for that period when she was on the verge of falling asleep every night. At times like that she didn't have a whole lot of control over her mind.

And her mind kept whispering that making love with a man like Thad Creed might be unbelievably wonderful. He was strong without being aggressive—his shyness could make him sensitive. But most of all, he was so quietly, unmistakably masculine.

When Edy approached her with that "tell all" gleam in her eyes, Gioia knew there'd be no escaping, but she was determined not to bring up the subject of her... exaggerations.

"Well? What'd I tell you? Isn't he great?"

"You ought to know," said Gioia, impressed with her own impromptu cleverness.

"Listen, I want to know *everything*! Did he kiss you good night? Did you invite him inside? Did—"

"No and yes. Hand me that roll of paper towels, will you?"

"When are you seeing him again? You *are* seeing him again, aren't you? Mack wouldn't tell me a single thing! I heard Sandy was dating Bill Sawyer now, so you don't have anything to worry about there."

"Believe me, I'm not worried. Does this guy look a little off to you? He doesn't usually hide out under the pen shell that way."

"What impressed you most about him?"

"He's off his feed. Unless he's a she, and she's spawning. That would explain it."

"Not the fish, dodo—T.J.! What did you like best about him?"

"Oh, um, well, I suppose it was his eyes. You can tell a lot about people from their eyes. Yours, for instance—"

Edy strolled across the well-appointed waiting room to peer at herself in the mirror. "Really? What can you tell about me?"

"Oh... that you're curious. That you really like people. That you're basically a happy person and that you use an oil-based foundation under your eye shadow, which makes it crawl into the creases."

Gioia made her escape while Edy was frantically blotting her turquoise eyelids. Unfortunately Gioia couldn't escape her own thoughts so easily.

Sunday, after church, Gioia changed into her usual jeans, topping them off with a bulky stone-green sweater. After last week's rain the weather had turned decidedly cooler, and she'd hung up her favorite straw hat for the season, replacing it with a battered red fedora. Both hat and paisley band had faded until they were the color of old brick. It wasn't the color that was important, though; it was the width of the brim.

It had been her grandmother, the one who had left her the house, the one for whom she'd been named, who had told her years ago that a broad-brimmed hat could do wonders to disguise a long nose, a high forehead or bat-wing ears. Her nose was okay—a bit on the short side but nothing to be ashamed of—and her forehead was pretty ordinary, but her ears...

It wasn't that they were big. Actually, they were quite small, and nicely shaped. The trouble was, they stuck out from her head. On anyone it would be unfortunate, but on a girl who had shot up to almost six feet while she was still in a training bra, it was disastrous. Fortunately, as the eldest of eight children, she'd been too busy to worry much about either her height or her ears, especially since her twin brothers suffered from asthma. Bat-wing ears were nothing when your baby brothers were gasping for their very breath.

Collecting the remnants of her lunch, plus a few stale hamburger rolls, Gioia headed for Riverton's tiny municipal marina. She liked to think the ducks were expecting her, but the truth was, they were shameless beggars, willing to show off for anyone who might toss them a crumb.

So much for the balance of nature, she thought wryly half an hour later. "You guys wouldn't know how to live off the land if your lives depended on it," she told a particularly bold mallard drake. "Look at you! Don't you know too much wet bread will clog up your pipes?"

"Try corn," drawled a deep voice from behind her.

"I would if I—" Turning, she saw T.J.—that is, Thaddeus Creed. Wearing corduroys that had faded almost to white, a sweater that was equally colorless and a tweed jacket that looked as if it had been stored over the summer season in the trunk of a car, he seemed a lot more comfortable than he had in the suit and tie. "Hi, Thaddeus. Is that what you feed them?"

"I don't feed them anything, but corn would probably be better than bread. They're built pretty much like chickens on the inside, aren't they?"

"I suppose. Comparative anatomy isn't exactly my field." She was disturbed at the way her stomach was doing flip-flops. It couldn't be lunch, which meant it had to be him.

He was a lot better-looking than she remembered, but he still couldn't be termed handsome. He looked sort of tough and defensive on the outside, as if trying to cover for the fact that he was really a marshmallow.

Was Thad Creed a marshmallow? She thought not. In fact, she'd be willing to bet that his tough exterior covered an even tougher interior. Speaking of comparative anatomy.

He leaned one lean hip against a silvery piling and stared at the row of yachts bobbing gently on the slight chop. "That's right. Your line is painting and baking pies and feeding fish and ducks and plants."

"The ducks are a hobby. There's not a lot of money in duck feeding."

"You require a lot of money?"

"I require a lot of food, and that requires a lot of money."

"I noticed," he said dryly. "The food, that is."

Warily he smiled, and so did she. Hers was probably broader than his, because she smiled often and easily, but it couldn't have had anything like the effect on him that his did on her. She felt it all the way down to her rubber moccasins.

"You don't do that a whole lot, do you?" she ventured, knowing she should find some excuse to walk away before she did something supremely stupid. "Smile, that is."

"Not a whole lot, I guess. Why, did anything crack?"

Sitting down at the edge of the water, Gioia nibbled her bottom lip and stared out at the boats without really seeing them. The ducks continued to paddle around, begging for more, but when none was forthcoming, they all turned, as if at a hidden signal, and swam off.

"So much for friendship, guys. You just like me for what I can give you."

"Are you surprised?" Thad asked.

She shrugged. "Not really. We don't have a whole lot in common. I don't even speak their language."

Somehow she ended up telling him about her fish—about the spider crab who liked to adorn his shell with bits of seaweed and anything else he could attach. "He's so vain, it's funny. And the prettiest fish in the tank is so shy, he won't even come out to eat when someone's watching."

"You really enjoy it, don't you? How'd you get involved in so many different things?"

"Necessity, mostly." The wind had picked up. It was raw and damp, and blowing directly across Thad toward her. She caught the hint of a scent that was enticingly masculine, and she was pretty sure it wasn't cologne.

No, she thought a few minutes later on her way home, having taken her own advice to leave before she fell any deeper under his spell. Thad Creed didn't need cologne or designer suits or fancy sports cars to work his magic for him. Whatever it was that he had going for him, it was subtle enough to have slipped up on her unexpectedly, and now she couldn't even look at the man without wondering what he would be like as a lover. Which was crazy enough. If he hung around much longer, she might even begin to wonder what he would be like as a permanent, till-death-do-us-part kind of lover. Which would not only be crazy—it would be downright dangerous!

She was under some kind of wicked spell. He had sprinkled something on her seafood. She wasn't the type to fall in love at first sight with a man she knew nothing at all about. It was absurd! Why, it wasn't even practical!

Three

───

Gioia knew immediately what the sickening wobble meant. Yesterday, when she'd been parked right next to a service station while she'd done the mall, it could have happened. Or the day before when she'd run around town half the day, delivering a cherry cream pie, a birthday cake and two dozen petit fours. But, oh, no, it had to wait until she'd removed the spare from her trunk in order to carry the extra set of sawhorses. It had to wait until she was on a job that took her seven miles out into the boonies, without so much as a farmhouse in sight!

Sighing heavily—it was either that or swear, and with seven younger siblings, she'd learned early to curb her tongue—she pulled off the road as far as possible and shut off the engine.

"What now?" she asked no one in particular. The gravel road dead-ended a mile or so beyond the old Timberlake house, which was her destination. Between where she was and the house there was only a dilapidated old marina, which was probably deserted.

Great. She could hike to the marina, and if they were open, she could rent a skiff, paddle home, collect her spare tire, ferry it back and then roll the blasted thing all the way back to the car. Just for starters!

This had *not* been her day. She'd awoken with a headache, thanks to a set of barometrically attuned sinuses, and then she'd broken the new glass replacement pot she'd just bought for her coffee maker.

It hadn't been her week, in fact. Her favorite seahorse had died. Something in the MacMillans' tank was devouring all the baby shrimp—she suspected the oyster toad, but she'd never caught him in the act. And to top it off, every plant in the Rappaports' conservatory except for the sansevieria was turning a nasty shade of yellow-brown, and she couldn't convince them it was too dry in there.

Of course, it hadn't helped that she'd been halfway expecting to hear from Thad—or T.J., as Edy insisted on calling him. It had been almost a week since she'd seen him at the marina, and she didn't even know why she'd expected him to call her. All she knew was that every time her phone rang, she broke her neck to reach it, and then had to swallow her disappointment when it turned out to be someone else.

"Hockey puck," she said succinctly, climbing out to see if the situation could be salvaged. Maybe it was a slow leak. She still had her tire pump. If she could pump it up just enough to get her to town...

But it was as flat as a flounder.

The first thing Thad saw when he rounded the curve was the buttercup-yellow Lincoln. There was no mistaking it. It was the same one that had taken up the entire length of

Gioia's driveway. He'd seen parade floats that were smaller, not to mention a hell of a lot more discreet.

"Need a hand?" he asked, lowering his window as he pulled up behind her.

"I'm not sure what a hand could do at this point." Her smile sort of wavered off into thin air, and she turned to stare dolefully at the crippled behemoth.

"Change a tire, for one thing."

"Great idea, if I happened to have a spare."

Thad bit back the comment he'd been about to make. From the look of her, she'd already gone through the entire routine. On the other hand, any woman who would travel an unpaved, deserted country road in a ten-year-old vehicle without a spare tire deserved a few words from an outside authority. And Thad just happened to have first-hand knowledge of dangers most civilians only read about.

He stepped out, nearly lost his footing in the mud, and slammed his door. He was impatient with Gioia Murphy, but even more impatient with himself for not being able to put her out of his mind. A woman he'd seen exactly twice in his life! She couldn't be more than twenty-two, and he was shoving hard at forty! Besides, she wasn't his type. He liked his women small, redheaded, mature and experienced enough not to look for more than he was offering.

So why the hell couldn't he get his mind off a kid with long black hair, witchy blue eyes and skyscraper legs? A girl who ate like a longshoreman and talked to ducks and smelled like wildflowers blooming in a pine forest?

"So what are you planning to do, apply for a land grant and start homesteading?" He hadn't meant to sound quite so scathing.

She blinked twice, and it was all he could do not to apologize. "Now why didn't I think of that? And here I was worried about a little old flat tire."

"There's a marina down the road a piece."

"I know. It doesn't look like much—probably just a worm-and-cane-pole place, but at least they might have a phone."

"Yeah, if they're open this time of year." Seeing her leaning back against the hood of her car, with her elbows bearing her weight and a scruffy-looking insulated vest riding up to reveal that ridiculously small waist of hers, Thad began to soften. Even dressed like that, without a scrap of makeup, she was stunning.

Damn it, he didn't *want* to soften! He'd earned his calluses the hard way, and he'd kept them for a very good reason—self-preservation. "Look, why don't I just drive you somewhere to pick up a spare, and then we can both get on with our own business?"

She appeared to study his offer, as if she had any real choice. Thad rammed his fists into his pockets and glared at the row of scraggly pines that separated a field of un-harvested soybeans from the Pasquotank River. Under a gunmetal sky the water was flat and colorless, the land-scape unremittingly drab. Gioia smiled, and it was like watching a Key West sunset.

"Get in," he growled. And then more gently, "Maybe you'd better lock your car. Anything valuable, put it in the trunk or take it with you."

"I've got cans of sealer and varnish and solvent—and my best brushes. I'd better take the brushes, but I can't see any thief lugging off gallons of varnish, can you?"

"Put 'em in the trunk. They'll be safer."

"No room. That's where I carry my sawhorse, which is why I had to take out the spare."

"Somehow I don't think the gentlemen in Detroit had sawhorses in mind when they designed this particular model," he observed with a twitch of the lips that almost resembled a smile.

It took the better part of an hour to go back to Riverton, wheel her spare out of the shed and wedge it into his trunk and return. By the time they got the flat off and the spare on, it was too late in the day for Gioia to start work.

"I'd better get rid of these supplies so I'll have the room for my spare tomorrow," she told Thad, who seemed reluctant to drive off and leave her. Her ears were still burning from the lecture she'd received when he'd seen the condition of her spare. She hated being lectured, and it was infinitely worse coming from him. Still, he'd meant well. "You don't have to wait, Thaddeus. I appreciate it, but..."

Damn the man! How could he disarm her without even saying a word? It was those eyes of his—and that stubborn, sweet, unhandsome face! "Okay, actually I'm glad you happened along. What on earth were you doing out here, anyway? There's nothing here except the old Timberlake house and the boat place."

"I, uh, had some time on my hands. I like to follow country roads, see where they lead, so I may as well tag along behind you in case the spare blows."

Fool! You're asking for trouble. If you're smart, you'll get the hell out of here and find some other way to check out that marina.

She gave him another two-hundred-watt smile, and he wiped a film of sweat off his forehead and watched her slide into her yellow battleship, drawing her left leg in just before she pulled the door shut. She'd been wearing the same paint-spattered sneakers the first time he'd seen her. They were even worse on closer examination than they'd looked from the road.

During the time it had taken to get the spare, return and change tires, Thad had plenty of time to examine in exquisite detail that slender, round-hipped, narrow-waisted body of hers. He swore softly. No woman should look that good in ragged jeans, a rope belt and an insulated vest worn over a faded red jersey that looked suspiciously like the north end of a set of long johns.

God knows it was a far cry from the way she'd looked the night of the dance. The tip of her nose was red, her hands were a real mess—even her hair was a mess. Her single braid was as shaggy as the winter coat on a banker pony, and she'd pulled a purple knit stocking cap down over her head. Not quite far enough, though, to hide a pair of small red ears that were poking through her glossy black hair.

All of which should have been enough to cool down his reactors; instead, he was about to have a core meltdown out here in the middle of a damn soybean farm, and all because of some kid who had no better sense than to go out on blind dates with men like his lecherous half brother!

Gioia led the way, whistling the "Triumphal March" from *Aïda*. She'd already made two trips to the Timberlake place—one to see if the woodwork was worth restoring, which it was. Quarter-cut oak, mahogany, cherry and rosewood. The oak was of a later origin, but the mahogany was Honduras, some of the boards nearly thirty inches wide. Both that and the cherry had achieved that wine-red color that was impossible to duplicate, and the rosewood was priceless. It would have been criminal to rip it all out and try to replace it with modern, manufactured stuff.

The second time, she'd brought out her power tools and a supply of steel wool and paper. Fortunately the power company had rigged a temporary pole so that the carpenters could get started. She'd already shot three rolls of film, documenting the condition the woodwork had been in before she tackled it, just in case a question arose later on.

Sometimes there was hidden damage that didn't show up immediately.

Thad helped her carry the heavy cans inside. "Who usually does the donkey work for you?"

"I do. Why?"

"The owner should provide someone to see to the heavy work." He placed the last can of sealer in the centrally located room she'd selected as her workroom, then flexed his fingers.

"I don't work directly for the owner. I'm a subcontractor. A lot of painters refuse to tackle this sort of thing. I'm going to have to rig some more lights in here, I expect," she said, gazing around at the dusty gray room that had once been a music room, according to old records. The humidity present in the outer rooms would have been lethal to the pianos or clavichords or whatever musical instruments had been housed here. "Ready to go?"

"I don't much like the idea of your working out here all by yourself," Thad said glumly. "Can't you hire an assistant?"

"Not if I want to clear enough to keep me in seafood platters."

"I see your point. All the same, you could get a dog, couldn't you?"

"You mean a guard dog? Like a Doberman or a German shepherd? Have you any idea how much those animals eat? I'd rather have a cat if I got anything. An attack tomcat." She grinned. "Come on, I'm getting cold. It's as damp as a tomb in here, isn't it?" she said cheerfully.

Thad watched her lock the massive front door and check the lock. Then he followed her out to her car, unable to keep his appreciative gaze off the shapely rear that swayed ever so subtly below the down-filled vest. He finally concluded that that walk of hers wasn't deliberate. It was something to do with her construction—her center of gravity, the width of her pelvis and the length of her legs. Not being an engineer, he didn't fully understand such things, but he could appreciate the results as much as the next man.

"I'll follow you home," he said.

"You don't have to do that. I'll stop on the way home and drop off my old tire to be fixed."

"I'll follow you, anyway, just in case."

"Well, okay, but only if you'll allow me to feed you. I made soup yesterday, and it's always better the second day. And I've still got half a cherry cream pie left. I'll never be able to finish it, because I have an order for a white fruit-cake, and I always bake two of my favorites."

"Must cut into your profits."

"It does," she said with a sigh as she slid under the steering wheel. "Unfortunately, I've got this awful sweet tooth and no resistance at all. My one vice, I think."

Nearing her home, Gioia tried to remember whether or not she had cleaned up the living room before she'd left. Or washed her breakfast dishes. Lunch had been two hot dogs and a coffee milk shake at Beau's Quicky, so the kitchen couldn't be too bad.

It was. Even worse than usual. She'd forgotten about dropping the lid to her coffee canister on the pot and breaking it. She'd cleaned up the worst of it with damp paper towels, meaning to mop as soon as she got home. Her toast was still in the toaster, looking limp and unappetizing. She'd been so disgusted with herself for breaking another coffeepot that she'd skipped breakfast altogether, which hadn't helped her headache, but it had justified the generous lunch.

"Sorry. I was in sort of a hurry this morning. Try the wing chair. It sits better than it looks."

Actually, it was a very comfortable chair, which is why she'd bought it at a yard sale. Of course, it had needed reupholstering, and that would have cost three times what she'd paid for the chair, so she'd done it herself. Sort of.

Thad was eyeing her art collection when she brought in a tray with two steaming bowls of black bean soup and a basket of piping hot corn muffins. Thank God for her microwave!

"That's kind of unusual, isn't it?" he asked, indicating an impressionistic—an *extremely* impressionistic—landscape.

"My brother Tave—Octavius, that is—did that when he was four. Daddy got him a set of watercolors because his asthma kept him inside so much. Trevor—that's the other twin—got a set of drums, but Mama took them away after the first day. She gave him a toy cook set that Angelica had never liked."

"Did they turn out to be artist and chef?" In spite of himself, Thad was fascinated by the idea that a family the size of hers should all be on speaking terms. It was rare in his experience. Far too much of his work, both on the force and off, had concerned domestic violence.

"Hardly. Eat your soup before it gets cold. I hope you like black bean. And there's marmalade for the muffins if you want it. They're already buttered."

Before Thad could tell her that he'd never tasted black bean soup, and butter was just fine, thanks, she went on to reveal that her brother Tave was studying aeronautical engineering on a scholarship.

"Thanks goodness for that," she told him. "As a school principal, Daddy's real big on higher education, but it's not easy to swing on his salary. You can imagine."

She didn't bother to add that with Trevor off at school, too, and the others growing up so fast, money was always an issue in the Murphy household.

Now and then Angie joked about finding herself a rich, generous husband to adopt them all. As the unrivaled beauty of the family, a petite blonde who melted the heart and eyeballs of every male who crossed her path, she could do it if anyone could. But money had never meant that much to Angie. She'd taken a short business course after high school and had immediately found work in the office of a local pediatrician. She'd always had a way with children.

"I'm not sure I can hold any pie," Thad confided after finishing the last muffin in the basket, as well as a second serving of soup.

"Just a taste, then," Gioia teased. "It's one of my bestsellers—my own recipe. There's a layer of cream cheese custard hidden in between two layers of cherries with swirls of sour cream on top. For Valentine's Day I bake it in a heart-shaped pan."

On Gioia's instructions Thad had dragged the lumpy wing chair over to the coffee table. She hadn't dared to invite him into the kitchen. She was going to have to improvise on the coffee making, but then improvisation was her forte. She might not be the most intellectual of the Murphys, but when it came to practicality she was the hands-down champion.

"You mentioned being in business for yourself, T.J., I mean, Thaddeus. Sorry, but my friend Edy—" And when he looked slightly puzzled, she said, "Edy Canfield—your friend Mack's wife. I see her several times a week, and she insists on calling you T.J., even after I told her you'd rather be called Thaddeus."

And then she felt a slow heat begin to steal up from under her thermal weave shirt. Drat! Now he'd know she'd been talking about him behind his back. Men hated that sort of thing! "I mean, she only asked about you once or twice—if I'd seen you since the night of the dance, that's all."

You're doing just great, pal. Open wide, insert foot.

"Gioia, listen. I'm not T.J. I'm Thaddeus A. T.J.'s my half brother, and about the dance, well, something came up at the last minute and he couldn't make it and, um, I came to explain, but—Well, you seemed to think I was T.J., and I just thought it might be easier to go along than to try to explain about the mix-up."

Thad raked a hand through his hair. He looked embarrassed, miserable and thoroughly irresistible. It was all Gioia could do not to reach out and comfort him. Physically. "Oh," she said softly, and her lips lingered on the word.

"I'm sorry. It was a lousy idea. I don't know what made me do it."

After the initial moment of shock, Gioia began to smile. And then the smile grew into a grin, and the grin erupted into a chuckle, and she flopped back against the sofa cushions and laughed until her eyes filled with tears. No wonder nothing had checked out! Tall, blond and handsome? And allergic to seafood!

When she could catch her breath, she leaned forward, her elbows planted squarely on her knees. She was still grinning, her eyes sparkling at the thought of how confused she'd been. "Tell me something, Thad, do you like to read?"

"Read? Well, sure I like to read, but what does—"

"Does T.J.?"

"Sure. *GQ, Playboy*...he's a real Garfield fan."

"And music. Do you like music?"

"I've got every tape Don Williams ever made, and I once stood in line for four hours to get into a Judds concert."

She subdued a hiccup and wiped her wet eyes. "John Williams? Well, yes, but who is Judds?"

"Not who is—who are. There are two of them, mother and daughter. And it's Don, not John."

"Oh. Well, what about Pavarotti? And Perlman?"

"Never heard of them. They must be new."

She swallowed the last of her smile. What else could she do? "It's been a real comedy of errors from the first, hasn't it?"

"Well, I don't know that I'd describe it exactly as a comedy," Thad ventured.

"Depends on your point of view, I suppose." Easing herself out from behind the coffee table, Gioia stood and reached for the remains of their supper, but Thad beat her to it. Their hands met on the tray, and she was aware of a feeling she hadn't felt in a long, long time.

Like maybe never.

"Sit," she said, her voice huskier than usual. "I'll make coffee. You do drink coffee, don't you?" She'd served water with the meal, needing time to figure out what to use as a pot. With her luck, he'd be a tea drinker, and there wasn't a tea bag in the house.

"Do you like wine?" she asked on a note of inspiration. A client had given her two bottles of Bordeaux left over from a rehearsal dinner in appreciation of the special effort she'd made to locate a tiny biplane to go on top of the cake.

"I'm not much on wine. How about beer?"

She flung out her hands in a gesture of helplessness. "Sorry. Never could abide the stuff. It's coffee, wine or Ovaltine."

Laughter glinted in Thad's deep-set hazel eyes, although no sign of a smile marred the straight line of his lips. "Coffee would be fine. Thanks. I'll help." He started to rise, and she shook her head frantically.

"Oh, no, I . . . you . . . that is . . ."

"You moonlight as a moonshiner. Between pies, paint and plants, you operate a still in your kitchen, right?"

"No, but it's an idea." Having given up on hiding her less than perfect housekeeping from him, she allowed him to bring the tray. "Watch where you step. I broke a coffeepot in here this morning and I haven't had time to clean up."

But it wasn't the smear on the white tile floor that drew his attention, nor the limp slices in the toaster, nor the dishes in the sink. "Rogues' gallery?" he ventured, stopping before the lineup of family photographs.

"Meet the Murphys. Mama and Daddy in the silver frame. Stasia when she was two. And the eleven-by-fourteen is Angelica. Then there's the twins in their senior year—Daddy held them down while I took the picture, because for their school picture that year Tave wore a red wig and Trevor parted his hair in the middle and colored it with black shoe polish. Mama almost killed them. The one on the pony is Rutherford. He's called Shoe at his own request. Don't ask me why. I reckon he was scared to death that someone would call him Ruth. Then there's Chloe and Mona and Stasia in their party dresses on Chloe's birthday, and that's the lot. Except for Bear. That's his rear end disappearing in disgrace around the corner of the garage in the birthday shot. He got to the cake first."

Thad continued to study the lineup on the dry sink while Gioia located a pot that would fit under her coffee maker and started the machine brewing. It hadn't escaped her that he lingered longest over Angelica's picture. Hardly surprising, she thought wryly. What man in his right mind wouldn't?

She turned her thoughts deliberately away from old wounds and got out her best cups and saucers. They were too small to be practical, but too lovely not to use. Her grandmother had left her the dishes and some fine old linens along with the house. The silver had gone to Angelica, the collection of books, old pin cushions, ship models and outdated farm equipment had been divided among the rest of the family.

"Do you take cream and sugar?" she asked. Turning away from the photographs—rather reluctantly, Gioia fancied—Thad shook his head.

"Black is fine," he said, lifting his thick dark eyebrows at the delicate violet-sprigged china.

They carried the coffee back into the living room, and somehow, neither of them seemed to be able to think of anything else to say. Gioia stared at Thad's hands, so square and strong and masculine as they held the tiny cup and saucer. He was square and strong and masculine all over, she decided. Square jaw, square hands, square shoulders. As for his strength, she had only to look at him to know he could take care of himself in almost any situation.

All at once, Gioia realized she was thoroughly tired of always being the strong one, always the practical one. It came of being the eldest of such a mob, no doubt, but suddenly, the urge to lean on someone stronger was almost irresistible. And Thaddeus was immensely strong, in his own quiet and very special way.

Blinking, she realized that her gaze had settled directly in his lap. He'd taken the wing chair again, his muscular thighs spread apart so that there was no doubting his masculinity.

She could feel the heat rise to her face. "Oh, for Pete's sake," she mumbled, gulping the last swallow of coffee, which went down the wrong way. Coughing and gasping for breath, she pressed her palms to her burning cheeks as her eyes blurred with tears.

"Hey, ease up. Let me take this before you drop it." The cup was removed from her hand and then he was beside her on the couch, drawing her limp body against his chest as he whacked her on the back. "You're not supposed to inhale the stuff," he muttered.

"Sorry. Whew! I guess you can tell I'm not used to drinking," she gasped, knowing she should pull away but unable to find the strength. Or the willpower. "Give me a minute and I'll be as good as new."

"It's all right. Take your time." The hand that had been thumping had begun to move in a lazy circle, sliding the thick cotton material over her skin. Her face pressed against his shoulder, Gioia filled her lungs with the scent of good wool, laundry soap and something more elusive—something more masculine. Something that threatened to knock every iota of common sense she possessed clean out into the stratosphere.

It was as if a shimmering mirage had enclosed them together, suspended in time, in space. Very deliberately Thad lifted her left hand and placed it over his chest. "There," he said deeply. "You see what you do to me?"

Gioia could no more help curling her fingers against his chest than she could help breathing. His heart was thudding under her palm, and she felt herself lean closer until she could see the tiny glints of light in his eyes, the almost invisible scar at one side of his chin.

Kiss me, damn it! What are you waiting for?

Are you nuts, woman? You don't even know this man!

And then Thaddeus lifted his own hand, just as deliberately, and placed it over her left breast. Oddly enough there was nothing sexual in the gesture, yet her pulse rate instantly doubled. From the waist down she went suddenly boneless, liquid.

He removed his hand as gently as he'd put it there, leaving her flesh burning in its wake. "Sure beats aerobics, doesn't it?"

Stunned at his offhanded manner, she turned to stare across the room. What was he doing with her? Trying to prove something? All right, he'd proved it! Whatever it was.

This was ridiculous. She hadn't reacted this way since those awful, endless days of metamorphosis known as adolescence, when she'd sworn to become a nun after a boy in her history class had told everyone she was a lousy kisser just because she'd beaten him on a test.

She'd never even held his hand, much less kissed him. With the help of a level head and a sense of humor that had been well developed even then, she'd gotten through it. Since then she'd learned to take emotional earthquakes in stride.

"I'm afraid your coffee's cold, but then it's a little late for caffeine." *Get out of here and let me figure out what it is you do to me, damn it! I've got to be able to look at you without wanting to slip off your clothes and find out what's underneath all those layers of flannel and corduroy.*

"Yeah, that's right," he said. "I've got some calls to make, anyway."

Perversely her spirits plummeted. "Thank you again for coming to my rescue."

"Forget it. Just don't drive without a spare again, even if you have to lash it on top. Is that clear?"

"No, sir. Yes, sir. I promise, sir."

Against all odds, he noticed a gleam of amusement light her eyes. "And don't be such a smartass," he growled with just the threat of a smile on his stern face. He didn't look directly at her. Nor did he bother putting on his jacket as he let himself out.

"No, sir," she whispered, leaning in the doorway to watch as he strode out to the muddy dark green Ford.

Thad got as far as his car and stopped. His mind had already ceased to function halfway across the porch, or he'd never have done what he was about to do now. But, damn it, sometimes a man had to act on impulse to avoid getting ulcers!

Or so he told himself as he marched back to the orange house, up the front steps, across the wooden porch and swept the waiting woman into his arms.

Gioia couldn't have uttered a word if her life had depended on it. She stood rooted to the spot while he hauled her roughly against his rock-ribbed body and proceeded to kiss her until the flesh all but melted off her bones.

After that first wild moment there was nothing particularly forceful about the way he was holding her. She could have pulled away if she'd really tried, but the sweet coercion of his lips, the tentative touch of his tongue, and most of all, the groan that emerged from his throat as he shifted his stance to align their bodies more closely...

She was lost. That was all there was to it. Lost and gone forever, dreadful sorry Clementine.

Four

Gioia had always prided herself on being levelheaded. She was the only natural-born pragmatist of the Murphy clan, most of whose members tended toward impulsiveness at best, recklessness at worst. During her freshman year at college, she'd fallen utterly and immediately in love for the first time in her life. His name had been John Pirelli, and he'd been an artist.

Had she panicked? Had she eloped? Had she flown into a grand tizzy and done something that might have ruined her entire life?

Hardly. Tizzies weren't her style. Instead, she'd held off moving into John's studio apartment until she could take him home with her to meet her family. Including Angie.

The end of her first and only major love affair had been quick and merciful. She'd survived it because she'd had no other choice. Subconsciously she must have been prepared for it; otherwise she would never have insisted on the meeting in the first place. It wasn't Angie's fault that every man who laid eyes on her immediately forgot that any other woman existed.

Poor John. He hadn't stood a chance, but she'd had to know. Angie had invented an excuse to visit a friend in Charlotte for the rest of the holiday, but it wouldn't have mattered if she'd stayed. Except that Gioia would probably have done something stupid and made matters even worse than they were.

John had been special—at least she'd thought so at the time. He'd been three inches taller than she, and they'd shared remarkably similar tastes in food, music, books, even the weather. They'd both loved rainy days when they could hole up with pizza, wine, books and a stack of good records. John had raved over her looks, calling her elegant, rare, poetry in motion. She hadn't recognized the cliché at the time, but had merely considered him far more sensitive and discerning than any other man in the world.

But elegance and poetry in motion had been no match for a cute, cuddly little body and a pair of aquamarine eyes that could stop a tank at fifty feet.

Gioia didn't blame Angie. You don't blame a person for an accident of birth, and Angie could no more help being irresistible than she could help being tone deaf. All things considered, the family gene pool had been pretty evenly distributed among the eight Murphy offspring. Some had talent, but were a bit short on common sense; others had brains, but no special talent; some had looks and some had cleverness. Gioia liked to think that her own special gift was practicality. She'd been the one to come up with the idea of scouring yard sales for almost-gems, refinishing and refurbishing and reselling at a profit. It had been fun, and she'd learned an awful lot about wood finishing and restoring, although she'd never quite mastered upholstering.

She'd also been the one to start the food co-op that had made the wholesale buying of groceries practical, and although she'd ended up doing most of the buying, hauling and bookkeeping, that, too, had been a learning experience.

Angie's special gift, aside from her startling beauty, was her way with children. She'd taken over Gioia's family baby-sitting duties as soon as she'd been old enough, allowing Gioia to start working toward her college education, and when she was no longer needed for that, she'd found a job in the office of a pediatrician.

Not even her worse enemy, if she'd ever had one, could deny that Angie Murphy was every bit as lovely on the inside as she was on the outside. It was hardly her fault that every single boy Gioia had ever fallen for from the seventh grade to her first year in college had defected after one look at her younger sister. Being a realist, Gioia had done what had been necessary: she'd left home, moving some three hundred miles east. And although no one in the family, to her knowledge, had ever discussed the matter, she had a sneaking suspicion that that was one of the reasons Granny G. had left her the house, because otherwise it was practically valueless. The realtor she'd seen when she'd first come to town had told her the chances to sell, or even to rent it out, were all but nonexistent.

"Practical?" Gioia muttered under her breath. For a practical woman she was having the devil's own time getting anything accomplished. So far she'd managed to spill an entire pint of milk when the carton slipped out of her hand, drop a raw egg on the floor and misplace her car keys.

First things first, she told herself as she firmly put Thad Creed out of her mind for the hundredth time since he'd knocked her lopsided by kissing her that way.

She sprinkled salt on the egg on the floor, scowled at the white dribbles on the wall over the sink and counter and emptied the milk from the soap dish. Then she wandered into the bathroom and peered at her face, angling one way and then another to see if she looked any different.

Why on earth had he kissed her? What had he been trying to prove? She'd begun to think that anything between them was purely a matter of her own overactive imagination. Their one and only date had been a misunderstanding. They'd bumped into each other at the marina, and then she'd had the flat and he'd helped her. So what did it all mean?

Oh, quit trying to analyze everything to death, she grumbled at her image—just because you're a Virgo! It was simply something men did, that was all. A conditioned reflex to any halfway decent-looking woman. He'd probably been trying to find out if she was easy or not, since he'd already invested a seafood dinner and a lot of mileage in her. If he'd bothered to ask, she could have told him the answer.

She wasn't *impossible*—under the right circumstances she could be pretty romantic—but she certainly wasn't easy. She had far better sense than to fall into bed with any man who beckoned. Not that he'd actually beckoned.

On the other hand...

The phone rang, and Gioia hurried to answer, glad of an excuse to cut short the soul-searching. She was already more than an hour late getting started this morning, and she had the mall and two office buildings to do, as well as a birthday cake for an octogenarian.

"Gioia, this is Thad. Are you busy tonight? What I mean is, if you'd like to have dinner, uh . . ."

Suddenly her palms were damp. Her stomach tightened into a hard knot, and she was having trouble untangling her brain.

Taking a deep, calming breath, she said with all the poise of a twenty-seven-year-old woman who had lived on her own for six years, "Gee, Thad. If I didn't, I mean, I have this, uh . . . cake?" Oh, Lord, brain failure! Her circulation had shut down from the neck up. Already scenes from the past were beginning to flash before her eyes. For instance, she could recall in exquisite detail the way his mouth had felt when it had first touched hers.

The kiss had been hard, almost rough at first, with noses mashed and something hard and rectangular in his coat pocket jabbing into her right breast. But then, seemingly with no conscious effort, they'd slid into alignment. Something magic had happened. Something soft and sweet yet as hot as fire, something that caressed and excited, stimulated and soothed. Something that had worked its way insidiously into her bloodstream so that when he'd released her she'd nearly fallen.

Looking as if he'd been poleaxed, Thad had stared at her without speaking a single word. And then he'd turned and left. When his car had disappeared, she'd still stood there, too dazed to go inside.

"That's all right. It was just an idea," Thad mumbled, and Gioia was suddenly terrified that he was going to hang up and she'd never see or hear from him again.

"No, look, why don't you come over here for supper? I could grill a couple of steaks or something while the cake's baking. It's going to take hours to decorate it, but you could stay and maybe talk to me, or we could listen to music. Or something."

Preferably *something*, she thought, and immediately made an effort to get herself under control. She was beginning to feel feverish. If she wasn't careful, she'd find herself in deep trouble again, and this time there would be no Angie to play Pied Piper and save her from making a fool of herself over a man who was only passing the time.

"You're sure it's all right?" he asked.

"I'm sure." She'd never been more sure of anything in her life. Or less sure.

"Great. I'll bring the steaks and the beer and, ah, what kind of wine do you like with your steak?"

"Never mind. I'd better finish off that Bordeaux first. Or maybe I'll have a beer."

That had been an incredibly stupid thing to say. Maybe she'd have a beer. In other words, maybe she'd bend herself out of shape trying to be what he wanted her to be.

She replaced the receiver and said, "Hockey pucks!" Stalking into the kitchen, she scooped up the egg, which the salt had more or less solidified, and then got out the mop. At least her kitchen would be spotless when he saw it the next time.

Thad straightened out one leg and then another, plucking his muddy jeans away from his knees. He wriggled his toes in an effort to get the blood circulating in his feet once more. He'd been crouched down in the damn bushes for hours now, waiting for a chance to get into the large shed that was part of the run-down marina. There were a couple of sailboats stored inside; he could see the tips of the masts above the corrugated metal roof. Unfortunately there was also a curl of smoke issuing from a stovepipe jutting crookedly out of a window, and a muddy pickup truck complete with gun rack parked close to the personnel door. It would be an ideal place to hide until the heat was off, or until a meeting with a buyer could be arranged. A yacht like that, Thad figured, should net the thief about a hundred grand, his only cost being a few cans of paint, a new set of sails, mooring fees and a set of forged papers. Not to mention a few bribes.

She *had* to be somewhere around here! He'd mapped out the possibilities and put out the word. If she'd gotten as far north as Virginia, he'd have known it. Unless she'd doubled back, she had to be somewhere within a radius of fifty miles or so. The trouble was that those miles included too many hiding places, and Thad was running out of time. For reasons of his own, the owner of the *Belle Star*, a stockbroker named Con Summerfield, had decided against calling in the Bureau. Someone had recommended Thad to him, and it had looked like a simple job of find, prove, hold.

But after nearly a month he hadn't caught a damn thing except a head cold and a case of poison ivy that had driven him crazy for a week down in south Georgia. Twice he'd almost had her, but she'd managed to slip away before he could get close enough to verify his suspicions, much less to board her to get proof.

The guy was as wily as a fox, and Thad was pretty sure he'd gotten a fix on him that time in Southport when he'd managed to get himself invited to a party aboard the yacht moored alongside the *Belle Star*—which had been calling herself the *Starfish* at that time.

Summerfield was getting itchy. If he called in the Bureau, not only Thad's pride and pocketbook would be hurt, but his professional reputation would be shot to hell. And in his line of work a good rep was everything.

She *had* to be around here somewhere! And he had to find her. He'd already invested too much time on this job, most of it doing just what he was doing now—waiting, and watching. And as miserable and boring as that could be, he preferred it to mingling with the Palm Beach yachting crowd in order to pick up information while trying not to get seasick whenever he set foot on one of those fancy, floating tax shelters.

Still, even that hadn't been quite as bad as the topless bar down in Georgia, where he'd found himself backed into a corner by three members of a female motorcycle gang who'd taken offense when he'd declined their offer to party. He'd had to talk fast to get away with his body intact.

Suddenly Thad dropped back down on all fours. The door to the shed had just opened and a man in hunting gear had come out and climbed into the pickup. Hot damn! He'd been about to call it quits for the day, but it looked as if his five-hour vigil was about to pay off. If nothing more, at least he'd soon be able to mark this place off his list of possibilities.

He didn't move a muscle. He hardly even breathed. This time of year the cover was sparse, and he was a little too close for comfort. "Come on, guy, get a move on. My feet aren't even on speaking terms with me anymore!"

The engine caught, choked, then backfired. Thad swore. The starter grated and the engine turned over sluggishly, then finally took heart. Just as Thad was easing himself out of his cramped position, the door of the metal shed opened again. A burly man in bib overalls and shirtsleeves waved his arms. "Hey, Elmo, get some Cheese Doodles, too, will you? And make mine chocolate milk instead of Mountain Dew."

Thad expressed his feelings with blistering directness as he began to back cautiously out of the thicket. The only cover he'd been able to find had been a patch of catclaw briers. Even if he escaped without catching pneumonia, he'd probably be scarred for life.

It was almost six by the time he got back to T.J.'s apartment. His half brother had just stepped out of the shower, having used, as Thad soon discovered, the entire supply of hot water.

"Thanks a lot, buddy," he grumbled.

"Hey, how am I supposed to know what your plans are? You're out of here before I even wake up in the morning, gone all day, and when I do happen to run into you, you can't even spare a civil word. No wonder Jackie bailed out on you. Unless a woman happens to be into suffering, she'd have—"

"Leave my ex-wife out of this." Thad's voice was without inflection, his eyes the color of tarnished metal and every bit as soft. Men had been known to grovel before such a look.

"Hey, sorry. Just kidding, okay? Look, if you're not doing anything tonight, why don't you come along to this party with me?"

"No thanks."

"Ah, c'mon, Thad, for old times' sake. What do you say? Jeannie's invited a few friends over—one more won't matter to her. The more the merrier, right?"

"What happened to what's her name—Sandy's replacement?"

"Gigi? Nice girl. Real sweet. She's got one of those whatchamacallits—hope chests? Parked right at the foot of her bed."

Thad peeled off his wet socks, grimaced at the sight of his pale, wrinkled toes and stepped gingerly into the bathroom while there was still a ghost of steamy warmth left over from T.J.'s shower. "One of these days they're going to take a long look at your receding hairline and you'll be wondering where they all disappeared to."

"Receding?" Frowning, T.J. peered at the full-length mirror. He'd always considered his high forehead a mark of distinction. "Receding? Hey, you're blind, you know that? Not only blind, you're insanely jealous."

Behind the half-closed door, Thad stripped off his briefs and was immediately covered in goose bumps. He turned on the hot water faucet full blast, got a limp stream of lukewarm water and, in colorful language, described the lineage of the contractor who had converted T.J.'s boat house loft into an apartment without bothering to insulate the walls.

"Why the hell don't you get a decent place to live in?" he called out over the drone of the shower.

"Don't knock it, man! It's got atmosphere, it's a great address, women love it, and it's cheap. What more can a guy ask?"

Thad didn't bother to reply. He showered in record time, pulled on a black knit shirt and a pair of tan twill pants and then dug through his suitcase, which he'd never gotten around to unpacking, for socks and a sweater.

"Change your mind about going with me?" T.J. was trying on sport coats from his tightly packed closet. Discarding a pale blue suede, he selected a navy blue blazer and studied the effect. "What do you think? Too dressy? Nah, blue brings out the bronze in my tan."

"God, you're a vain son of a bitch, aren't you? Look, I'm going out to dinner, but I'll be back early. Then I'll probably be going out again. So if you happen to get in first, don't wait up for me, okay?"

"Whoa, man! What's this dinner thing? And what's with the after-shave? You're not going on a stakeout reeking like a musk-ox, are you?"

"I happen to have a dinner date. Afterward, I thought I might check out that boat house again. Those jerks have got to knock off and go home sometime."

"Forget the boat house. What's with the dinner date? I didn't know you even knew any women around here."

"Butt out, will you? I'm in a hurry. And what the hell did you do with my other shoes?"

"Under the sofa. Who is she? That redheaded clerk down at Beau's Quicky? How'd you talk her into going out with you? It sure can't be your pretty face, big brother. What did you do, give her a three-hanky job about how your wife ran out on you when your life was hanging by a thread and—" He jumped back, hands lifted defensively. "Hey, just kidding, just kidding! Not the nose, Thad! Dad swore if I ever broke it again, he wouldn't lift a hand to fix it!"

Slowly Thad's fists uncurled. Whether or not he would actually have landed one, he didn't know. He'd never struck his brother, although he'd been provoked more than once. They didn't get along—never had. Sometimes Thad wondered why he even bothered to maintain the relationship. He was pretty sure T.J. wouldn't go out of his way to look him up if it were left up to him.

"Okay, but lay off my private life, you hear? Who I see and what I do is none of your damn business. If it bugs you to have me here, I'll get a room in a motel. Probably be better, anyway."

T.J.'s look of consternation was too good to be faked. Thad had had years of experience reading faces, gestures—words spoken as well as those not spoken. "Ah, forget it. I was just ticked off because I spent the whole damn day up to my armpits in mud and briers, waiting for some turkey to go home to his grits and greens and let me get a look in his boat house."

"You think you've found the *Belle* what's it?"

"How would I know? The place was occupied all day and there aren't any damn windows." He'd told T.J. no more than was necessary about the case that had brought him to the northeast corner of North Carolina. He'd had to have some excuse to hang around. If he was going to use his brother for cover, common decency as well as common sense made it necessary for T.J. to know what was up. At least enough so he wouldn't open his mouth at the wrong time in front of the wrong people.

"Sorry about the hot water. If I'd known you had a date..."

T.J.'s smile held something of the same self-deprecatory charm that had made Thad bail him out of trouble again and again over the years. They'd grown up in separate households, separate towns and definitely in separate social and financial circles, but they'd kept in touch. Thad had stopped seeing his father years before he'd decided to enter the police academy. Thad Senior had been in the throes of his second divorce at the time, with wife number three, who was scarcely older than his eldest son, waiting in the wings.

"No problem," Thad finally said. "Maybe starting out the evening with a cold shower's not such a bad idea."

Gioia tried on the yellow polyester dress that looked just like silk. Her bed was littered with the contents of her closet. Nothing was right. She had jeans, and she had really dressy stuff, but very little in between. At least nothing she liked. Suddenly everything she owned was dowdy and dull and entirely too practical.

Except for the yellow dress, and even that was machine washable.

She'd wear jeans. It was no big deal. Besides, she was going to be working. She still had that birthday cake to finish, and she wasn't looking forward to creating a miniature duck blind complete with decoys in colored frosting.

The jeans fitted her like a glove. She put on her best black turtleneck and her red ballet shoes, then drew her hair back with a red silk scarf, artfully arranged to disguise her ears. There was nothing illegal about making the most of your assets, she told herself—or the least of your faults.

She was ready way too early, and she made herself get to work on the cake. Creaming and beating brought a becoming flush to her face, and soon she was humming. She'd always been able to lose herself in baking. By the time she heard Thad's footsteps on the porch, the cake was in the oven, filling the house with a heavenly smell. But the flush remained, and along with it a noticeable sparkle in her eyes.

Thad stood in the doorway and stared for a full minute. For once in her life Gioia was completely tongue-tied. He was so handsome! No, she amended—even better than handsome. His was a face that revealed character, strength and reliability, all traits she admired. His nose might not be Roman, but it was a fine nose, and his eyes were truly lovely.

As for his *lips*! She blinked and then took herself in hand. "You can come in if you want to," she invited. Her smile felt as brittle as spun sugar. When he brushed against her before she could move away, she suddenly felt as weak as if she hadn't eaten in days. In all her twenty-seven years she had never been so aware of another person. Maybe she was coming down with something!

"Are those the steaks?" she asked, desperately struggling for composure.

"Steaks. Oh, yeah, these are the steaks." He shoved them at her and then snatched them back. "I'll carry them for you. They're, uh, wet. I mean cold. Oh, hell, the beer. I'll be right back."

By the time they finally got settled in her sparkling clean kitchen, Gioia had herself more or less under control. Really, she was going to have to do something about her social life. If she was so out of practice that she couldn't even invite a man to dinner without coming unglued, she was in deep trouble.

Thad didn't seem all that much better off. "That's the cake," he observed, nodding at the three square layers she had hurried back to the kitchen to remove. They were now turned bottom up on the cooling racks. "It's, uh, all finished, then."

"Hardly. The birthday boy wants lemon filling and coconut frosting, with a hunting scene on top. I thought I'd do blue water with coconut whitecaps, a caramel marsh and maybe a chocolate duck blind with lots of tiny little decoys all around. What do you think? Too much?"

"You mean people eat that sort of thing?" he asked, then reached out and blotted up a crumb with his forefinger.

Gioia watched him lick it off. He had nice fingers. He had nice hands. In fact, everything about him was nice in a tough, weathered sort of way. "Sure people eat it. I bake delicious cakes."

"Did you bake an extra one?"

"No, but I've still got some of the white fruitcake left. I froze half of it. I've got pie, too."

"Sweets aren't supposed to be good for you." The words were spoken absently, as if his mind wasn't on what he was saying.

Gioia felt just as distracted, but she covered it well. "I know. I try to eat lots of wholesome stuff, too, to make up for it."

As if that revelation were an invitation, Thad's gaze moved over her, from the top of her gleaming blue-black hair, with the red scarf, to the black jersey that accentuated her small, high breasts, to the length of rope she wore in lieu of a belt. "Flat knot," he said aloud, and she nodded and swallowed hard. "Do much sailing?"

"No, but I'm great with a canoe as long as nobody moves."

"I get seasick," Thad confessed. He scowled, as if wishing he hadn't said it, but the small confidence seemed to break the ice.

They both began to talk. Gioia told him all about the boat her grandfather had spent the past eighteen years of his life building. It was still in the garage because it was too big to come out, and besides, no one trusted it not to sink. "The only boat he'd ever owned was a battered old skiff with a three-horsepower outboard, but he used to love sea stories. He'd stay up all night to watch an old World War II submarine movie."

Thad told her about an incident that had happened shortly after he'd first joined the police force. "This old fellow had made arrangements to be buried in his car—it was a vintage Packard and didn't have more than a hundred miles on it. He'd taken care of it as if it were some kind of shrine."

"I've never seen a Packard," Gioia admitted. She popped a pair of well-scrubbed potatoes into the oven and took a sip of wine. It was a bit dry for her taste.

"Yeah, well, it seemed one of the grandsons had been dealing drugs and was using the car as a place to hide the stuff. We got a call one night that someone was digging up a grave, and by the time we got it all sorted out, the kid was in custody, the narcotics division had made a record bust and the old lady got an offer you wouldn't believe for the car."

"She didn't take it, of course."

"Sure she took it. Wouldn't you?"

"Not if I'd truly loved him. Would you?"

"Damn right," he said.

But somehow she knew he was lying. There was something essentially tender about Thad Creed. Yes, tender was the right word. It was there, even though he went to great lengths to cover it up with his tough-guy act.

Neither of them seemed to be able to find anything else to say until Gioia jumped up with a nervous laugh. "I'd better get the fire started if we're going to eat tonight." She flung open the back door and began noisily dragging the grill out onto the back stoop.

Thad followed her out. "Get inside. I'll do this," he ordered. He was still wearing a fisherman's knit sweater over a black knit shirt, although he'd taken off his shaggy tweed jacket. "You're shivering already. Where do you keep your charcoal?"

She was shivering all right, only it wasn't entirely from the cold. When he'd brushed past her, his arm had seemed to linger on her back for the tiniest fraction of a second. It had been long enough to kindle that peculiar incendiary thing that happened to her every time he touched her.

Was he going to kiss her again? Oh, please...

What was she thinking of? All he'd done was offer to light her fire. *Oh, Lord, did he ever light her fire!*

Enough of this foolishness, she chided herself, digging under the storage compartment for the lighter fluid. The man was only passing through town—visiting his brother, or so he'd said. And while Gioia had enjoyed her share of casual kisses—because under the right circumstances kissing could be a pleasurable thing to do—she wasn't sure she wanted to get involved in *that* sort of thing with Thad Creed. It had been her experience that there were two basic kinds of kisses. There was the "thank you for a lovely evening" type that you shared with a man when you liked him well enough to spend a few hours in his company, even though neither of you were interested in taking things to stage two.

And then there was the other kind. John Pirelli's first kiss had been that kind. Boom! From stage one to stage three in one second flat.

She handed Thad the can and then watched as he heaped the briquettes and doused them with the lighter fluid. His back was to her, but she could see his hands, the deft way they moved. No wasted motion at all. He was a quiet, efficient man, almost too self-contained. She didn't know the first thing about him, not really. She only knew that the very first kiss she'd shared with Thad had taken her well beyond stage three, and she couldn't afford another one, because for some reason that she was at a loss to understand, she was extremely vulnerable to this man. One more kiss and she might come down with something terminal.

Like love.

Gioia made up her mind on the spot. Tonight would be it. End of the line. They would eat and talk and then she would concentrate on decorating her cake. After a while, when he decided it was time to leave, she'd make sure she was involved with an intricate bit of work, so that he could let himself out. And that, she thought to herself, would be the end of it. No more kisses, no more complications.

That was definitely the way to play it. These exotic fly-by-night types, no matter how attractive, were totally impractical. When and if she found a man who could pass the Angelica test, she might think about getting seriously involved, because she didn't particularly want to spend the rest of her life alone. But she had far better sense than to get mixed up with a man like Thad Creed. A man who appeared out of nowhere, managed to wipe out every one of her defenses without firing a single shot and then rode off into the sunset. Alone.

Gazing with naked longing at the man who was watching the flames leap up almost to the porch roof, she sighed. There were times when being practical could be a royal pain, and that was the truth.

Five

The rest of the evening dutifully followed the guidelines Gioia had set, right up to the point where the wind picked up and she jumped up from the table and hurried out to put the cover on the grill in case a few live coals blew out.

Thad called after her, wanting to know what was going on, and she yelled back for him to pour the coffee, that she'd be right back. She had closed the top of the cast aluminum smoker-grill and was crouched over, tapping shut the bottom draft with a stick of wood, when he came after her. The stoop was scarcely big enough to turn around on and the grill sat square in the middle. The back door swung open, hitting her on her backside, and she flung up a defensive hand.

It all seemed to happen at once—the bump, the burn, her scream and his grabbing her around the hips and pulling her away from the hot grill. Her hand had caught one fringed end of her scarf, ripping it off, her hair was flying everywhere in the gusty wind, and Gioia felt her knees buckle as the first wave of pain hit her.

"Where? How bad?" Thad demanded, easing her down onto the floor. "Your hand? Your face? Oh, God, look at me, Joy. Let me see!"

Within moments she managed to get hold of herself. The pain tightened her stomach like a hard fist, but she'd had kitchen burns before. Occupational hazard. "My hand...just my hand," she gasped.

"Let me see."

She was sitting and he was kneeling partly beside her, partly behind her. Braced in the cradle of his thighs, she allowed herself to lean against him, just for an instant. Just until she could catch her breath.

"I feel...greenish," she said with a shaky laugh. He was holding her wrist, frowning down at the angry red blemish that ran all the way from the wrist to the tip of her little finger on the outer edge of her right hand.

"Let's get some ice on this."

"Butter?"

"Cold water. Then maybe something else. Come on, can you stand up?"

"It's my hand, not my foot. Of course I can stand up."

But by the time she was up, she was ready to sit down again.

He held her around the waist, watching her like a hawk. "Okay?" he asked, his concern siphoning what little strength she had left.

"Just a few butterflies. I hate pain. It gives me a woozy stomach."

"Shock. Don't worry about it. It'll pass." He helped her into the kitchen, supporting the arm with the injured hand. She felt like a dreadful phony, especially as she was even more aware of the hard body that was bracing hers than she was of the hand that ached all the way up to her arm-pit.

She brushed her face against his shoulder to get the hair out of her eyes. Lord knows where her scarf was by now—probably halfway to the next county. Thad led her over to the sink and held her hand under a stream of cold water, and gradually the pain began to diminish until it was little more than a heavy throb. His chest was pressed against her back, his thighs against her thighs. He circled her wrist with steely fingers as if they were handcuffs and she were his prisoner.

A lock of hair slithered over her shoulder and fell across her cheek, and she used her left hand to brush it aside. One of these days she was going to get it cut short. She really was. Ears or no ears. Neck or no neck.

She felt Thad's free hand on the back of her head, stroking her hair, her scalp. He mumbled something that sounded like "Black silk," and then she felt his fingers brush her nape. She shivered. It was just the shock, of course—from the burn, not his touch.

"Thanks for the water cure," she said a little breath-lessly. "The pain's almost gone." That was a slight exag-geration, but she needed some space. Having him pressed against her this way, holding her hair in one hand and her wrist in the other, with his warm breath fanning her cheek, was doing more harm than good. She was beginning to unravel, and she simply had to put an end to it before it went any farther.

"Okay, let's look you over. If the skin's broken, I'll drive you to the emergency room. Can't be too careful with burns."

Gioia dropped down onto the kitchen chair that he held for her, grateful to be off her feet. She was beginning to feel giddy, which wasn't at all like her. "Stop smothering me, will you? I do this all the time. Well, not all the time, but often enough. Cuts. Burns. Stuff. And, anyway, the hospital is way out on the other side of Elizabeth City, and I hate hospitals, and the skin's not broken. I've had worse sunburns than this. I'll be just fine."

"Tell me where you keep your first-aid supplies and I'll fix it up for you."

She told him, wondering frantically whether or not her underwear was still hanging over the shower rod. Oh, what difference did it make, she thought impatiently as she leaned forward to brace her arms on her thighs. He was back before she could catch her breath, with a jar of petroleum jelly and a box of surgical gauze that had probably been in the back of the medicine chest since World War I.

"I don't need a bandage."

"You'll end up wiping this gunk off every time you make a move if you don't cover it with something. Have you got any old gloves?"

"Rubber, wool, canvas or pigskin. Take your pick."

"Forget it." He knelt before her, taking her wrist in his hand and frowning over the shiny red streak that marred the whole outer edge of her right hand. "Pretend you're King Tut for a few days."

"Did you ever watch King Tut decorate a cake? Or clean out an aquarium? Or repot a ficus?"

Thad grunted noncommittally, his attention on the job of smoothing a film of Vaseline over the reddened area. Glumly, Gioia stared down at his hair, noticing the gray strands that mingled with a hundred shades of brown to produce a color that was impossible to describe. His hair grew low on the back of his neck. It looked remarkably soft, for all its thick vitality.

She sighed. Thad leaned back and wiped his hands on a handkerchief that was obviously pristine, and just as obviously unironed. He stuffed it back into his pocket and screwed the lid on the jar. "Okay, Tut, let's get you into the living room where you can lie down. I'll fix you something hot and sweet to drink and—"

"I'll take coffee. No sugar, no cream."

"You'll take it sweet. Shock does something to your system. You can get hypoglycemic."

"What are you, a doctor?"

"Ex-cop. Be surprised how many times you run into shock in that line of work."

She was flabbergasted. She would never have guessed, yet now that he'd told her, it seemed to fit so well. That tight-lipped control of his for one thing. The innate kindness he tried to cover up with a layer of toughness a yard thick. She'd never cared much for macho, but Thad exemplified macho at its best. Now she was beginning to understand why.

"You said *ex*," she reminded him, inviting an explanation.

"I'd better get the coffee." He was gathering up the first-aid supplies when she yanked at his sweater with her good hand.

"Darn it, Thad, *talk* to me!"

"I thought we were talking. You want a mug or a cup?"

In other words, she thought, butt out of my private life, lady. Feeling raw and irritable, Gioia snapped, "A cup if I have to drink it sweet. You're so damn smug, aren't you?"

That stopped him in his tracks. "Smug?"

"About your piddling little secrets. For your information, I was only being polite. I couldn't care less if you're

a shoe salesman or a ballet dancer, much less how you got
to be an ex anything. Far be it from me to pry!''

"What the bloody hell are you going on about,
woman?'' Spinning on his heel, Thad strode back to where
she lay on the sofa. He slapped the back of his hand across
her forehead. "You running a fever?''

"No, I am not running a fever! What I am running
is . . . what I am is . . ." To her horror, Gioia felt the tip of
her nose turn red. Her chin began quivering and her eyes
filled, and unthinking, she made a fist with her right hand,
lifting it to wipe away the tears. The sharp pain took her
by surprise, and it was the last straw.

Thad was beside her in an instant. He gathered her in his
arms, and like a beached jellyfish, she lay there, dribbling
tears of sheer frustration all over his shoulder.

He was murmuring words that made little sense, com-
forting words, the kind you might say to a child. It had the
perverse effect of making her cry all the harder. And the
worst part was that she was afraid to stop, because once
she did, he'd turn her loose, and there was no way she
could hide, and her face was ruined, and her ears were
poking through her hair, and. . . "I'm sorry," she sobbed.
"It . . . it's the cake.''

"The cake," Thad repeated, thoroughly baffled.
Everything about this whole business had him buffal-
oed—the woman, most of all. He'd rendered first aid to
any number of people, both in the line of duty and outside it, and not one had affected him this way. He could
feel the pain in her hand, feel the thickness in her throat,
as if it were his own. *Why?*

Damn it, he was starting to get involved, and that was
the one thing he'd sworn never to do again. Of course, that
didn't mean he didn't want to sleep with her. Hell, she'd
had him in a state of almost constant arousal since the time

he'd leaned over to pick up his napkin and seen those long, silky legs of hers that went all the way from here to *there*!

But that was sex. Pure, simple, uncomplicated sex. Thad was no eunuch, but like most men with half a brain who'd been through the grinder a few times, he had a deep-seated aversion to involvement. Involvement was like quicksand. Involvement with a woman like Gioia was more on the order of the La Brea tar pits.

How the devil had it happened? He'd come by to apologize and to make some excuse for T.J., and then he'd seen her sitting there on her front porch swing with that bit of fluff around her shoulders and her hair shining like obsidian, and she'd looked so...

Okay, so he'd taken her out. One of the Creeds had owed her something, and the other one was an irresponsible jerk. That would have been that, but then he'd run into her a few times, seen her around town and, well, hell! She was good to look at. She walked as if she were hearing her own private music in her head, and he'd always been a sucker for a woman who moved well. What's more, she didn't take herself too seriously. She could make him smile. Hell, she could make him laugh! No one had made him laugh in such a long time that he'd almost forgotten how.

But the worst part—the part that made him know he had to get out while he still could—was that it felt so good to hold her, to take care of her, to blot up her tears with his collar.

And if that wasn't a clear signal to save his hide while there was still time, he didn't know what was. "Look, the cake can wait," he told her. "By tomorrow you'll be able to use your hand a little bit."

"No, it can't wait! I have to deliver it to the nursing home at nine o'clock tomorrow. And the decorations have to set, or they'll droop when I take it out, because it's supposed to be rainy."

"Okay, so I'll help you!" *Going, going, gone.* "There, that's settled. Now stop crying and blow your nose. I'll get the coffee, and after that we'll tackle that cake."

He dug out his rumpled handkerchief again and pressed it into her good hand. The burned one was resting on his shoulder, feeling so good that it was downright scary.

The coffee was strong, and he'd laced hers with three spoonfuls of sugar and a stiff shot of brandy. Gioia made a face. "You used the good stuff," she accused.

"Not all that good. What the devil do you keep it for if not for an occasion like this?"

"For my baking, and it *is* good. It might not be Courvoisier, but it wasn't cheap."

"So charge extra for your birthday cakes and make up the difference."

"It's for the pecan pies. Some people like them with brandy and some with bourbon."

Thad grinned and dragged over a footstool to sit on. "I'm beginning to understand why you've got such a following. I hope you've got a license for peddling that stuff."

He'd brought her a mug, not a cup. She set it down on the end table. "Any alcohol I use for flavoring is long gone before I deliver my goods. Well, maybe the fruitcake... You sound just like an ex-policeman."

Thad handed her back her mug. "Drink it. All of it."

It was simpler to comply than to argue. "It's like drinking preserves."

"With your sweet tooth? Come on, quit being so contrary."

"I don't like *everything* sweet. I enjoy contrasts. Bitter, sweet, tart, hot."

"I'll take sweet, tart and hot," he said, and his eyes met hers and held until she could scarcely get her breath.

Suddenly self-conscious, Gioia sat upright and lowered her feet to the floor. She brushed ineffectually at her hair and said, "I must look like a scarecrow."

"You don't look all that bad. Your nose is a little red and your eyes are kind of swollen and blotchy, but on the whole you don't look too bad."

"I could do a good job of hating a man like you," she grumbled. "What is it with policemen? Do they take some kind of oath to tell the whole truth and nothing but the truth? Thanks a lot." The fingers of her left hand strayed up to fluff out her hair at the sides.

He grinned, and she felt herself relenting. How could she stay angry with a man who changed her flat and greased her burn and even offered to decorate her cake? In fact, she didn't even know why she was so upset with him. What difference did it make what he thought of her?

All right, so it made a difference. So she wanted him to tell her she was beautiful, even when she cried and that haystack was his favorite hairstyle, and that her swollen, blotchy eyes reminded him of sapphires. And as long as she was dreaming, she might as well have him tell her that the good Lord had chosen to make her ears so prominent only because it would be a crime for such shell-like perfection to go unnoticed.

"Hockey pucks."

"What?"

"Look, this has been lovely, but I've got to get to work. If you'll just drag my basket out for me, I can handle the rest." She stood up too quickly and swayed on her feet.

"You're nuts, you know that? You're not up to doing that damn cake tonight."

"Don't be silly. Of course I'm up to it."

"One shot of brandy and you're knee-walking drunk."

"Altitude sickness," she said with a shrug. "When you're as tall as I am, it takes a while for your blood to get up to your brain. Any sudden moves—"

"Don't give me that. You were dizzy. I told you I'd trim your damn cake for you. It might surprise you to know that I majored in modeling clay in kindergarten."

"What surprises me is that you were ever a child. Tough guys like you . . ."

When she didn't finish, he lifted one brow, the expression in his eyes clearly daring her to finish it. "Known a lot of tough guys like me, have you?"

There weren't any more like him. She'd have felt it in her bones if she'd ever come within ten miles of another Thaddeus Creed, tough guy supreme, ex-cop, and ex Lord knows what else. But she didn't say it. She wasn't up to matching wits with him tonight, or any other night.

"Forget it. If you want to help do the cake, I can't stop you, but quit fussing at me, you hear? I don't like it and I won't tolerate it."

"My mama said you could always tell a lady by her unfailingly gracious manners."

With a cutting look that told him what he could do with his "gracious manners," Gioia led the way to the kitchen. Her hand was throbbing, her head was reeling, and fair or not, she was inclined to blame him for both maladies. Wisely she pounced on something more tangible. "You used practically a whole roll of gauze on one teeny burn. I feel like I'm getting ready to enter the boxing ring!"

"You're lucky I don't take you up on that," he muttered. "Where's the stuff?"

"Under there." She jabbed a thumb at the cabinet where she stored her baking materials. "The yellow one."

He perused the row of pastel laundry baskets and took out the yellow one, setting it on the table. "Color-coded filing system, I suppose. What's in the others?"

"Pink is cake makings, blue is bread makings, white is pie crust and yellow is frosting."

"What are you, some kind of efficiency expert?"

The look he gave her was tinged with respect. At least Gioia chose to interpret it that way. "I see no point in wasting time and energy chasing all over the kitchen whenever I start to bake. This way I have everything I need, and I can tell at a glance when something is getting low, so I replace it before it runs out."

"And this is the only job you could find around here? With all your talent, I'm surprised some big corporation hasn't snapped you up."

Much of the tension that had unaccountably sprung up between them had eased, but Gioia was still feeling edgy. Using her left hand, plus the thumb and forefinger of her right, she began assembling ingredients. "In case you haven't noticed, there's not a whole lot of industry in Riverton. Slide that mixer over here, will you?"

"So move. You're not stuck here, are you?"

"My house is here."

"Rent it. Sell it. Board it up."

"Nobody wants it, and my grandmother left it to me, and what difference does it make to you, anyway? Plug it in, please."

"Maybe one of your dozen or so brothers or sisters would like to move in for a while."

"There's only seven, and they don't. Riverton isn't exactly the hub of the universe, and what difference does it make to you, anyway? I don't see you breaking your neck at whatever it is you do. Are you laid off? Or on vacation? What *do* you do now that you're an ex, anyway?"

She sent him a look of grim satisfaction as she rolled a lemon on the table. He wasn't the only one who could pry.

"At the moment I'm combining business with pleasure, you might say. You want me to slice that thing for you?"

Getting answers out of Thad Creed was like cracking black walnuts: hardly worth the effort. "No, I want you to scrape off about a teaspoon of the rind and then squeeze the juice into that measuring cup for me."

They worked surprisingly well as a team, and by the time Gioia was instructing Thad on the art of reshaping chocolate and caramel drops into tiny decoys, he had learned that she'd once dreamed of being an opera singer, that she read romances and how-to-books, liked cats better than dogs, was crazy about all kinds of seafood and had a beautiful sister who somehow intimidated her.

That last bit of information he'd figured out for himself. It would be the one on the end—the busty little blonde in the white bikini who knew how to point a toe for the cameraman to make her legs look sexier.

"There's so much fascinating stuff to choose from," Gioia said earnestly, transferring a smear of confectioner's sugar from cheek to black shirt with her bandaged fist.

She was talking about her plans for the future. Thad was much more interested in her present, because he knew he wasn't going to be around long enough to figure in her future.

"You know, I've always been sort of interested in learning more about astronomy," she continued. "But I understand there aren't too many job opportunities in the field, so it doesn't make much sense to waste all that time and money on something that won't pay dividends. A business major is more practical, especially when you go to college the way I do—work a year or so, take a few courses . . . and so on."

"How old are you, anyway? Twenty-two? Twenty-three?"

She pinched another coconut whitecap in place and sent him a sidelong grin, her eyes as dark as blueberries. "Flattery will get you a pan to lick out. Filling or frosting?"

"How old?"

"Cad. I was twenty-seven last September."

Thad finished the last decoy. No way did it look like any bird he'd ever seen, but she seemed satisfied with his efforts. Twenty-seven. She looked a lot younger. She would look a lot younger when she was ninety. It was her expression, mostly—like a light that shined from the inside out.

Twenty-seven. She was almost eleven years younger than he was. Even younger than that in experience, unless he missed his guess. And he rarely did about that sort of thing.

With an apparently casual interest, he allowed his gaze to wander over her, coming to rest on a pair of small pink ears that she seemed embarrassed by, but which he found damn near irresistible. Technically speaking, he'd known far more beautiful woman. Certainly far more suitable ones for what was on his mind—not that it seemed to matter. His body had turned on to her practically from the first good look, and there didn't seem to be much he could do about it.

Other than get the hell out of here while he was still able.

So what was he doing hanging around? Angrily he licked a smear of chocolate off his thumb. He had about as much business messing around with a woman like Gioia Murphy as he did chasing a stolen ketch from Florida all the way to God knows where!

A good deal less, in fact. He might not have the legs, the stomach or the inclinations of a sailor, but he was a damn good detective. He was closing in on a criminal no one else had been able to bring down.

Gioia was another matter. He should have told her flat out that T.J. wasn't going to make it and left it at that. For a man who'd sworn off all but the most superficial relationships with women, he was asking for trouble. Besides, she wasn't the kind of woman for a casual fling. She was a keeper, and he wasn't into keeping, which meant he needed to get out of her life and stay out before she got hurt. The very fact that he cared more for her well-being than for his own pleasure was just one more danger signal.

"Time I was shoving off," he said, unstraddling the chair and hooking a thumb under the sweater he'd removed earlier. "Anything I can do before I go?" He told himself it wasn't disappointment he'd seen on her face before it had gone carefully blank.

Gioia leaned over to place a caramel decoy near the chocolate blind. "Thanks, but you've already done more than enough. I'd have been at this all night if you hadn't helped out. What do you think? Pretty convincing, isn't it? Especially if you squint at it."

"Take away the old guy's glasses before you hand it over."

She followed him through to the living room where he collected his jacket. They didn't look at each other, and the silence was as brittle as an icicle. They'd just spent nearly three hours laughing together, arguing the merits of country music over classical, beer over wine, cats over dogs, and even Mexican food, which was Thad's big weakness, over seafood, which was hers.

He didn't kiss her. He said nothing at all about seeing her again. Just as he climbed into his car, Gioia remembered that there were two bottles of beer left in her refrigerator, and she opened her mouth to call out to him, and then closed it again.

Stalemate. That was the way she thought of it over the next few days, although she tried not to think of it at all. Or of him, for all the good it did.

On her way out to the Timberlake place on Wednesday, she saw a dark green Ford that looked exactly like Thad's, but of course dark green Fords weren't all that uncommon. This one was parked at the edge of the woods about halfway between the marina and the house. Hunters, she supposed.

She couldn't see the license plate for the mud and tall grass, not that it would have done her any good, anyway. She couldn't even remember her own license number. She always got it mixed up with her social security number.

The new roof was almost finished and the drywall was coming along, which meant the painters and paperers would be right on schedule. That is, they would be if the heating and plumbing crew ever finished getting the duct work installed for the new furnace. The last tenants had relied on oil heaters in all the major rooms and a wood stove in the kitchen, which had done nothing at all for the interior walls. She'd scrubbed tons of soot off before she could even begin to start removing old paint and varnish.

She'd brought along her tape player, and a few of her favorite tapes. Bundled in long johns, jeans, a wool stocking cap and her insulated vest, she worked cheerfully all morning. At least she told herself she was cheerful. She was singing along with *Don Pasquale*, wasn't she? Wasn't that proof enough?

Instead of eating the cheese and bean sprout sandwich she'd brought with her, Gioia opted to drive back to town for a pizza, a milk shake and maybe an order of fries. Sanding was hard work, she rationalized. Besides, she needed to get out and breathe some fresh air after being cooped up in a dusty room all morning.

The green Ford was gone, but there was a beautiful sailboat moving sedately up the creek. This time of year there was very little boat traffic, especially this far upriver. She cut the engine and watched. It was a gorgeous day, with sun glinting off the water, and the sky almost royal blue shading to smoky lavender. More rain in the offing, judging from the mackerel clouds, but for now it was perfect.

"One of these days," she promised herself. Gioia had a long list of one-of-these-days wishes. One of them was to travel. She'd grown up in a small town in central North Carolina, traveled once to Washington, D.C., on her senior trip, and once to Mobile, Alabama, to be maid of honor at a cousin's wedding. Other than that, zilch. She'd gone to the University of North Carolina in Charlotte because it had been only an hour or so from home. Practically commuting distance.

Moving from Silasville to Riverton had been an adventure, and it had given her a taste of further adventures. One of these days she was going to do something totally impractical. Hop a train across the country, or go on one of those scrumptious-sounding sailboat charters in the Caribbean. Or maybe fly to Alaska. She had a cousin in Kodiak.

Sighing, she started the car again. The sailboat was out of sight now. Evidently it was bound for that ratty-looking marina, unless it belonged to one of the nice houses farther up the river. Not too much farther, at that, or the railroad bridge would clip the top off its tall, shiny mast.

By the time she finished her five-minute personal pan pizza with everything and then some on top, Gioia had forgotten the sailboat. She was mulling over whether or not to call Thad and remind him that she had two bottles of beer that belonged to him and that she just happened to have a pot of chili going to waste.

She would make the chili and then decide. After leaving the pizza place, she stopped by the market and bought the ingredients, raced home and started it cooking. Then she drove back out to the Timberlake house. She was determined to get all but one layer of old finish off before the painters started in the front room. They had a running battle over who would splatter whom, but time was on her side. She could afford a bit of strategic dawdling, whereas they had more jobs all contracted and waiting.

It was almost five when she got home, which was practically night at that time of year. She was cold, exhausted and half inclined not to bother calling Thad. The chili would keep, and her hand was really throbbing. She'd given it a workout. She could do without Thad's smug "I told you so."

With her hand in a plastic bag, she managed a bath and shampoo, relying more on soaking than scrubbing. Swathing her hair in a towel, she topped off the tub with hot water and settled back to soak out a few more aches and pains. Ladder work always got her in the knees and thighs.

It wasn't so much a case of idle hands as an idle mind. No matter how hard she tried, she couldn't prevent her thoughts from straying back to Thad, and the last time she'd seen him. And the times before that. Silky, sensual images began to form as the bubbles cooled and popped around her—Thad on his knees beside the tub, his chest bare. Hairy? Mmmhmmm. Moderately hairy, with nipples the color of copper, and nice, firm—

"Hockey pucks," she grumbled, pulling the chain with her toe and levering herself out of the claw-footed tub. The phone rang while she was toweling off, and before she could get to it someone began pounding on her door.

Great. Just what she needed, an aluminum-siding salesman on the phone and Lord knows who-all at her front door! The last time it had been a trio of hunters, wanting to know who owned the fields surrounding her house. With her six bird feeders and a dozen or so windows in mind, she'd blithely told them that she did, and that it wasn't available for hunting, since she had several small children who played outdoors year-round.

Oh, Lord, they'd caught her in the lie and now they were coming to get her!

Grabbing the phone with her good hand, she tried to pull on her bathrobe over her wet body. Her hair was dripping down her back. "Hello!" she shouted, looking frantically in the direction of her front door. "Angie? What's wrong?"

"Does something have to be wrong for me to call you?"

"Look, hang on a minute, will you? There's someone at my front door." Gioia ignored the squawk or protest— Angie didn't like to be put off when she had something on her mind, a minor failing that Gioia had forgotten.

It was Thad. With a helpless, hopeless look Gioia let him in and then dashed back to the phone. Whatever he wanted, it could wait. Family took precedence, and Angie never called unless it was something important.

GET YOUR GIFTS FROM SILHOUETTE®
ABSOLUTELY FREE!

Mail this card today!

PLACE
JOKER
STICKER
HERE

PLAY THIS CARD RIGHT!

YES! Please send me my 4 Silhouette Desire® novels FREE along with my free Bracelet Watch and free mystery gift. I wish to receive all the benefits of the Silhouette Reader Service™ as explained on the opposite page.

(U-S-D-12/89) 225 CIS JAY3

NAME _____
(PLEASE PRINT)

ADDRESS _____ APT. ____

CITY _____

STATE _____ ZIP CODE _____

Offer limited to one per household and not valid to current Silhouette Desire subscribers. All orders subject to approval.

SILHOUETTE BOOKS "NO RISK" GUARANTEE

- There's no obligation to buy—and the free books remain yours to keep.
- You pay the low members-only price and receive books before they appear in stores.
- You may end your subscription anytime—just write and let us know or return any shipment to us at our cost.

IT'S NO JOKE!

MAIL THE POSTPAID CARD AND GET FREE GIFTS AND $10.00 WORTH OF SILHOUETTE NOVELS—FREE!

If offer card is missing, write to:
Silhouette Reader Service, P.O. Box 1867, Buffalo, NY 14269-1867

Six

―――

I'm on the phone. You'll have to excuse me," Gioia said, desperately trying to fasten her robe with her good hand. Already she could feel the wetness from her hair spreading over her back, but that small discomfort was the least of her worries. What was far more alarming was the way her body had reacted to the sight of that taut, muscular build, the high cheekbones and crooked nose, the steady eyes that seemed to look through her, discovering secrets she didn't even know she had.

"No, Angie, I didn't forget you." She gestured frantically toward the wing chair, and Thad sat. Slinging his left ankle over his right knee, he settled back with every appearance of comfort.

"Um, what was that? Your job? Oh, Angie, you didn't!" Deliberately she turned her back on her visitor and listened while her sister described just how miserable she was, and how she'd quit her job, and how no one at

home understood that she needed sympathy, not accusa-
tions.

"I knew you'd understand. In fact, I thought maybe,
just for a few days, I might come visit you. I could help
with your cooking and all that."

Angie was a wizard with children. In the kitchen she was
barely adequate. "Look, let me call you back later, okay?
I, uh, can't talk now."

"You have company?"

"Yes."

"A man?"

Brief hesitation, and then, "Yes."

"Oh, Gioia, tell me! Who is he? What's he like? Is he
spending the night?"

"No, he is *not spending the night*!" she practically
shouted. Then, aghast, she whispered tersely into the
phone, with Thad sitting not ten feet away, "I think he's
selling encyclopedias. I'd better show him out." She hung
up in the middle of a warning about allowing strange men
inside her home at this hour of the night. It was barely
seven o'clock.

"I have a great assortment of tapes out in my car," Thad
informed her with lazy amusement. "Everything from
Alabama to Zeke Saunders and His Blades of Grass. I'm
fresh out of encyclopedias, though."

"Sorry. I had to say something, and it was all I could
think of."

"How about, 'A friend just dropped by to see how I was
feeling'?"

"It didn't occur to me. Is that why you came?" Tuck-
ing her bare feet up beside her, she settled into one corner
of the couch and touched the opening of her peach-colored
chenille robe to be sure that it was securely closed.

"I was worried about your hand."

"It's just fine, as you can see." She waved the slightly grimy wad of gauze, and then wished she hadn't.

"Needs changing," he said, and he was out of his chair and beside her before she could think of a rebuttal.

"I was going to, that is, I *am* going to change it as soon as—"

"As soon as you get rid of your encyclopedia salesman?" He sank down on the cushion beside her and reached for her hand, and Gioia, slightly off balance because of the way she was sitting, was tilted toward his shoulder. "You got it damp," he accused.

"So now you're afraid I'll catch cold?" Her spine stiffened in an effort to hold her away from him. The springs of Granny G.'s old sofa weren't cooperating.

Thad began unwinding the gauze, and Gioia stared at his well-groomed nails. His square-tipped fingers, for all their tapered shapeliness, looked swarthy and dangerous against the vulnerable blue-white skin of her inner wrist. One of them brushed against her bare palm, and she drew in a deep, shuddering breath.

"Hurt?"

"No. That is, yes. Look, thanks for unwrapping me, but I can take it from here." Was it her imagination, or did his gaze stray to the front of her old bathrobe when she mentioned unwrapping?

It wasn't her imagination! He was staring directly at her bosom, as if he could see under all that thick, draped cotton chenille. Or even without it. And while she wasn't overtly endowed in that department, she wasn't normally so self-conscious, either.

"I've got to call my sister back," Gioia blurted. No point in wondering where *that* association had come from. As she'd told herself over and over, the gene pool had been fairly and evenly divided; Angie had gotten the curves, and she'd gotten the height. Chloe had an average figure and a voice like an angel. Mona was as lean as a whip, but she was a computer genius. And Stasia, even at thirteen, showed signs of becoming another Angie.

"Thad," she murmured, feeling a powerful need to remove herself from his presence before she did something supremely stupid.

"Mmmmm?" He lifted her hand and examined the red streak along its side.

There was only one blister, but it was a rather long one. Unfortunately it was right at the joint of her little finger, so that every time she forgot and moved it, it felt as if someone had branded her with a hot poker.

"I'd better, that is, you'd better, uh...go?" Great. That was certainly firm and authoritative enough to get him off his duff.

"I'm awfully sorry about this." He held her hand up close to his face, as if to examine it more closely, and she could feel his warm breath blowing over it. It was excruciating.

"It's not your fault." Smiling nervously, she tugged at her arm. He held fast. She tugged harder. He turned slightly, and suddenly she was sprawled across his chest, her injured hand held out as if they were waltzing. She grabbed at his shoulder with her other one. "Thad, what are you doing?"

"Hush. You needed this," he muttered. "No...I'm the one who needs it."

And then his lips touched hers in a beseeching kiss that drained every shred of resistance right out of her body. It was as though she absorbed the very essence of him through her pores. Taste, scent, texture, the soft tug of his teeth on her lower lip that opened her to a deeper invasion; it all combined to provoke a sensory overload. But that was only because she was tired, she told herself desperately as she felt her robe fall apart under Thad's skillful hands. Only because it had been so long since anyone had held her this way.

His palms were hard, his touch unbelievably gentle. When his thumb feathered lightly over the tip of her breast, making it rise like a small pink acorn, she moaned softly, burrowing her face in his throat. Somehow her burned hand had been placed out of harm's way on the back of the sofa, and both of his own had come into play, stroking her, holding her, tilting her head for another kiss.

"Thad, this isn't smart," she gasped, as powerless to resist him as steel was to resist a magnet.

"Shhh, nobody's checking your IQ."

She managed to put three inches between her lips and his and tried her best to look stern. "Don't be facetious. You had no business taking advantage of me, of my—"

"Of your handicap?"

She shrugged, not quite meeting his eyes for fear she'd seen laughter there. Or something even more dangerous to her equilibrium. Her IQ might not be all that outstanding, but her survival instincts were well honed. Every instinct told her she was precariously balanced on the edge of an abyss, and down was a long way to fall.

"Gioia, you're a grown woman. An attractive, decent, desirable woman with no ties and no encumbrances, according to your own testimony. I get the impression you tolerate my company. I know damn well I enjoy yours. So what's the hang-up?"

A sudden flush of gooseflesh along her thighs made her glance down, and to her horror she saw that her robe had fallen almost completely open when Thad had untied her sash. The only thing saving her modesty was the sash itself, artfully draped across her lap.

With a groan she grabbed for it, instinctively using her right hand. Pain lanced sharply up her arm, and she doubled over. "Oh, God, how did I ever get into this mess?"

Deliberately, and with a tenderness she could hardly credit, Thad folded the two flaps of her robe over her lap, smoothed the lapels up to her throat, and then drew her sash around her waist, tying it in a great, ugly bow. He looked so sweet in his concentration that she could have wept.

I could love this man, she heard a small internal voice whisper.

You've been hitting the vanilla extract again. This isn't love. It's unadulterated lust!

"Thank you," she whispered, and made the mistake of lifting her eyes to his.

She could see the dark centers expand. His face took on a look of harshness, and he drew in his breath sharply. "God, Joy—!"

She was in his arms, the lumpy bow pressed uncomfortably between them, and there was no force on heaven or earth that could have prevented what happened next.

Thad stood, drawing her to her feet. He swung her up into his arms, and the world tilted crazily. Gioia closed her eyes, her breath coming in shallow little gasps.

"Where are you taking me?"

"To bed . . . I hope."

It was a question, and Gioia saw her last chance flicker away like the shadow of a falling leaf. "I hope so, too."

By the time he reached the second floor, he was breathing hard, and she didn't know how much was due to her weight, and how much to other factors.

It was the other factor that took precedence, however, when he lowered her to the floor just inside the door of the room she'd indicated. He slid her down his body slowly—

so slowly it was a wonder she didn't keep right on sinking until she was nothing more than a puddle of liquid desire at his feet.

She had no more strength than warm candle wax—and not half the brains. She knew it. She refused to think about it. Not tonight.

Although the room was chilly, neither of them noticed. It could have snowed right through the ceiling and neither of them would have noticed.

Their eyes caught and held as Thad reached out and slid his hands underneath her robe, easing it from her shoulders. The loose sleeves fell from her arms, and it hung on the sash at her waist.

Gioia felt her nipples tighten as the cool air struck them. Thad's dark gaze was a palpable force—it was as though he were touching her, and all he was doing was staring.

"Oh, my," he whispered hoarsely.

"I'm too small..."

"You're perfect. You're so lovely. I've never seen any woman..." He halted abruptly. There were no other women. Had there ever been?

"I wasn't apologizing. I was just—that is, some people—"

His hands enclosed her small, pink-tipped breasts. He didn't squeeze. He didn't even caress her. He simply held her and stared into her eyes until Gioia uttered a small cry and then they were in each other's arms.

The sheets were icy cold. Somehow, Thad managed to get out of most of his clothes, and Gioia welcomed the heat of his body as he joined her on the bed.

His voice was husky—raw, almost, as he murmured broken words between kisses. He kissed her throat, her eyebrows, her temples, his lips brushing the dark silk of her hair, and then he returned to her lips.

"I haven't been able to get you out of my mind. It's like a slow poison." He moved, and his mouth was on her breast, and lightning streaked through her body, causing her to stiffen until the soles of her feet were pressed against the cold metal of the bedframe.

"P-poison?" She was having problems keeping her hands from exploring.

"The sweetest kind of poison." His laughter was something felt rather than heard. "The kind that drives a man wild and makes him love it." His warm palm circled lazily over her stomach, gradually moving lower.

Gioia was like a person in shock. Stunned by the depths of her own passion—her own need, she opened herself to his searching hands, and then gasped when he closed in on her most sensitive flesh.

What was happening to her? She wasn't like this! She had never been like this—never gone off like a—like a firecracker! "Please. I can't—stand—much—more of..."

It came on her suddenly, like a hard, hot summer rain. Like rainbows, dissolving and arching and dissolving and arching until she was nothing but a shimmering beam of white heat.

He watched her ecstasy, feeling great pride, and oddly enough, even greater humility that he had been the one to bring her this gift.

And then his own control broke, and he moved over her, and she welcomed him, and it began all over again.

A long time later—it seemed forever, but it had been less than an hour—Thad opened his eyes and studied the woman sleeping in his arms. It never should have happened, damn it. He'd promised himself that he wouldn't take matters this far—not with Gioia. That he'd get out before either of them could be hurt, and now he'd loused things up royally.

With wry humor, he wondered what the chances were of pretending he had amnesia. It never happened, honey—you must have me mixed up with some other man.

He sighed. For a supposedly intelligent guy, he had managed to pull some real blunders in his life, but this one was in a class by itself.

The phone rang. He groaned, not wanting to turn on a light. Not wanting to answer the thing. Not wanting to come down to earth.

Gioia mumbled something under her breath and snuggled closer, her thigh insinuating itself between his in a way that stiffened more than just his resolve. "Rise and shine, sweetheart."

"Tha's jus' my 'larm clock." Her eyes were still closed, those three inch lashes of hers spread out on her cheekbones like black silk fans.

"Better answer it, honey—it's your phone."

"'Larm clock. Hit it for me, hmmm? I've gotta three-day snooze alarm." But she was awake now. Reluctantly. "Oh, darn," she said, and began to ease away when the shrill ringing suddenly ceased.

"Okay, Tut, rise and shine and let's get you bandaged again. You break that blister, you're going to be in trouble. You probably need some kind of antibiotic stuff to keep from getting infected."

Gioia couldn't believe she was hearing what she was hearing. Her hand? After what had just happened, he was worried about her hand?

Thad sat up and leaned against the brass headboard, ignoring the way it bit into his back. Steeling himself to ignore the almost overwhelming urge to find the damned phone, rip it out by the roots and then spend the rest of the week in bed, making love to her, he reached for her right wrist.

"I'm just trying to be practical," he said, and she jerked her wrist out of his grip.

"Then as long as we're being practical, you might as well know that I didn't use any protection. I—it's not something I usually have to think about." Her bottom lip was sticking out belligerently. Unfortunately, it had a slight tendency to tremble.

He'd known she was inexperienced. Not totally, but whatever experience she'd had had been a long time ago, he suspected. His voice was gruff when he said, "Don't worry about it, Joy. I took care of it."

"I'm not worried, d-dammit! I—oh, would you just get out of my bed and go home?"

"Not until I take care of your hand," he replied calmly.

"I can take care of myself! I've been doing a reasonably good job of it for six years—longer than that!"

"Congratulations. Now—" He stood up, splendidly naked, and folded back the covers he'd pulled over them earlier. "Your hand?"

Wanting only to be rid of him so that she could set about determining what had made her go off the rails that way, Gioia stalked after him into the bathroom, pausing only to sweep up her bathrobe from the floor and ram her fists in the sleeves.

Her hand hurt like the very devil, and she welcomed the pain. She needed something to focus her mind on until she dared to face her own thoughts.

Dropping down onto the padded stool, she held up her hand. "Be quick about it if you don't mind. I have a lot to do tonight."

"About tonight, Joy..."

"And don't make it too tight around my wrist, will you? It might cut off the circulation." She kicked at a wet towel viciously with her foot, provoking no more than a lifted brow from Thaddeus, who was neatly winding about six miles of gauze around her hand. The bathroom was just as she'd left it when the phone and the front door had sounded at the same time—bath oil cap off, underwear dropped down behind the door, wet towel flung across the shower rod, and shampoo things on the edge of the sink.

Only now, he was in it, too, and it was different. Everything was different. "It won't happen again, you know."

He looked up at that, frowning distractedly. She couldn't believe a man could—could do something like that and then just get up and go about his business as if it were no more than a—a drink of water. "I hope not."

"You do?" She didn't know what sort of reaction she had expected, but that wasn't it.

"Yeah—most accidents happen in the home, you know. Women get to—"

She could have screamed. Would have, probably, if the phone hadn't started in again at that moment.

"Want me to get it?" Thad asked, finishing his task and setting aside the gauze.

"There's nothing wrong with my feet." She stood up so suddenly she almost tripped over the towel she had kicked aside.

"I—uh, left this number with my answering service. In case of an emergency," he called after.

By the time she got to the downstairs phone, she had fastened her robe more securely and regained a small portion of poise.

Which she promptly lost as Thad strolled downstairs in his jeans, carrying his shirt and shoes in his hands.

She snatched up the phone, glaring at him as she held it against her bosom. She told herself she was overreacting. She told herself that in a little while, she would regain her perspective, and everything would be just the same as it always was. Dull. Empty.

"It's for me," she said coolly. For heaven's sake, this sort of thing happened all the time. A man a woman met. Zap! Instant attraction. A full-blown, but totally meaningless, lust attack. As short-lived as a summer thunder squall.

"Angie again?"

Gioia tightened her lips and gestured pointedly at the door before turning her back on him to greet her sister.

"Has he gone yet?"

"No, he hasn't gone yet. I'm thinking of calling the exterminators."

"Gioia, is there something you're not telling me?"

"Nothing important. Look, Angie, if it's not too urgent, could we talk tomorrow? I could call you early, before I leave for work."

Meanwhile, Thad strolled around her living room, casually examining her collection of records, tapes, books, and still more family photographs. She should have burned that one of Angie, the twins and herself at the beach when she was fifteen!

She kept her back turned, but it didn't help. Aware of his every move, she listened abstractedly while Angie went on and on about someone named Jack, who had been having marital problems, and whose wife was ready to slap her with an alienation of affections suit, and honestly, none of it was her fault, but Gioia could see why she simply had to get away, because Daddy was mad at her and Mama kept looking at her and shaking her head, and everyone was talking, and her reputation would be ruined if Mrs. Loggins went through with it.

In the midst of all that, the doorbell rang. It took a moment to register, because no one ever used the bell. "Yes, of course I understand, honey, sometimes these things just happen," she said in her most soothing tone of voice while Thad answered her door, just as if he had every right. Thank goodness he had put on the rest of his clothes. It was bad enough that she was wearing nothing but a bathrobe, and suddenly her house had turned into Grand Central Station!

Sighing distractedly, Gioia began murmuring excuses to get away. She'd heard it all before—or variations of the same theme. It wasn't Angie's fault men simply couldn't resist her. Strangers had been known to follow her home after a single careless smile.

Angie was saying something about a rest, and needing to talk, and not being the least bit of trouble. Gioia lost the final thread of the conversation when an incredibly handsome man followed Thad into the room.

He was blond, tanned, and she decided on the spot that if he weren't a male model he definitely should be. Thad, looking darker and more forbidding than ever, was scowling. The newcomer was studying her with frank masculine interest, and Gioia was suddenly uncomfortably aware that her hair was in need of a thorough brushing, her lips were undoubtedly swollen, and the electricity that crackled in the room whenever she looked at Thad would be obvious to a dead man.

The front door slammed, and she blinked and said, "What? I'm sorry, Angie, what were you saying?" Thad had left! Without a word—after what had happened—! He had walked out and left her here alone with a perfect stranger. An exceptionally perfect stranger, but a stranger, nonetheless.

"I said I'll see you tomorrow. Tell me how to find you," Angie demanded. And with her brain racing around in seventeen concentric circles, Gioia did her feeble best.

Poor Angie—with her sense of direction, she'd probably wind up somewhere in West Texas. At this point Gioia didn't much care.

Where was Thad? Why had he raced out without even saying good-bye? And who on earth was this golden Adonis who was flexing his muscles all over her living room?

Clutching her five-year-old bathrobe around her throat, she told herself that no matter what, Thad wouldn't have gone off and left her alone with an ax murderer. Besides, no ax murderer worth his salt would risk getting blood all over that expensive white silk turtleneck and the crested navy blue blazer, would he? "I don't believe we've met," she said, making it sound like a world class faux pas on his part.

The smile he bestowed on her would have lit up a city block. Gioia was totally unmoved. "I'm T.J. Creed, and of course, you're Miss Murphy. Joy, isn't it?"

"Gioia." She spelled it out for him. "I suppose you're Thad's brother."

"Half brother, actually. Our mutual father enjoys variety."

She didn't know what to say next. Was there a polite way of asking what he was doing there?

She felt as if she had awakened onstage in the middle of a Kafka play. Without a script.

Manners, drilled into her by both parents during her formative years, came to her rescue. "Would you, ah—care for a cup of cake? I mean, coffee? That is, sit down, won't you?"

She didn't want him to sit down, she wanted him to get the heck out. She wanted him not to have appeared at all, and for Thad not to have left. And if that wasn't crazy, she didn't know what was.

"Thad said to tell you he had this call he had to return. Some guy says he's been trying to reach him all day at two different numbers, but either the line's been busy or there was no answer, so I thought I'd better deliver the message. I must say, I'm glad I did."

The mildly flattering remark and the openly admiring look only made her impatient. "Is he—that is, will he be—?" Coming back, she wanted to ask, but couldn't bring herself to voice the hope. "Nothing serious, I hope," she said instead.

"I doubt it. Some guy named Summerfield—something about insurance."

"Oh, good. I wasn't sure..."

"I know what you mean—in Thad's line of work, you never know."

"No, I don't suppose you do," murmured Gioia, wondering how she could discreetly pry into something that was none of her business.

"Yeah, I mean, one day he might be broiling his bacon on a beach in the West Indies, and the next, he'll be holed up in a hay barn in the middle of nowhere."

Her eyes widened. The effect was not lost on T.J., who decided that he might have been a bit hasty in his dismissal of this eccentric long-stemmed beauty. Carefully plucking at his creases first, and making certain the requisite amount of silk ankle showed between the bottom of his flannels and the top of his alligator shoes, he seated himself in the lumpy wing chair and set about drawing out the woman he'd once considered not worthy of his time and attention. "So...tell me about Gioia Murphy. Lovely name—is it a family name?"

"Murphy? Yes, it came down to me from my father."

He didn't crack a smile, must less laugh at her feeble attempt at a joke. Of course, Thad wouldn't have laughed, either, she reminded herself, but their eyes would have met, and his would have been dancing with golden highlights. It had happened enough times so that she'd begun to look for it. To invite it, even.

Instead, T.J. launched a rambling discourse on his own name, which happened to be a very ordinary one. "The Thomas Jackson I was named for made his first ten million before he was forty. Got out of western oil and into eastern real estate just at the right time. Timing's everything, you know."

Gioia's stomach growled, reminding her that it was going on eight o'clock and she usually dined to the tune of the six o'clock news. "Speaking of time..."

"For instance, I happened to know that the manager of the place where I work is thinking of retiring early next year. The way I figure it, with all the development practically on our doorstep, Elizabeth City's going to be a goldmine in the not too distant future. Thad thinks I'm pretty dim, but I've got this idea..."

And on and on and on. Gioia's eyes glazed. Her stomach rumbled ominously. If Adonis didn't shut up and leave, she was going to be forced to invite him to do both. So much for gracious manners.

"Thad thinks I'm a real lightweight, you know? I mean, just because I've changed jobs a few times—well, a guy has to look around, you know? I mean, I'm not content to just sit back and wait for opportunity to knock on my door. A guy's gotta move around, find out where the real opportunities are. The way I figure, you don't look in the big cities—they're already overrun. Find a nice small town, I told myself—somewhere close to a growing resort area. A place that's on the move, not one that's already peaked. Then get in on the ground floor of a good, recession-resistant business, and you've got it made, right?"

"Right," Gioia said weakly. "Speaking of Thad," she began, but he was off again. The difference was that this time she listened, her hunger forgotten.

"Old Thad wouldn't know opportunity if it sent him an engraved invitation. Too stubborn—always was. Only reason he joined the police force was to bug the old man. He could've finished college. Dad would've paid. But that would've been too easy. That might've let the old man off the hook for walking out on Annie—that's Thad's mother. He was just a kid, but don't think he ever forgot and forgave. Not his style, you know what I mean?"

Suddenly, Gioia felt acutely uncomfortable. As much as she wanted to know everything there was to know about the tough, introverted man who seemed unwilling to share a single particle of himself, she didn't want to learn it this way. If Thad wanted her to know, he would tell her.

"Have you been here very long? You're not from this part of the state, are you?"

"From Virginia, originally, near Richmond. There was this woman I met—Sandy Shoemaker, but that's another story."

"Mmm, yes. Pity it's so late. Maybe another time..."

"Another—? Oh. Yeah." Reluctantly he stood, twitching his shoulders to assure that his jacket would fall correctly. "Sorry. I didn't mean to bore you."

Then of course, she had to assure him that she hadn't been bored, but perhaps he was more perceptive than she'd given him credit for, because he said, "A word of advice—don't knock country music or Louis L'Amour. Oh, yeah—and don't expect him to take you dancing. Ever since he took those bullets in the back, he's been afraid to try it. I keep telling him, if he can crawl around in the mud on all fours and chase some creep three and a half miles at a dead run, he's not ready to be put out to pasture yet, but you know how it is. Some men have too much pride, and ever since his wife walked out when he was still in intensive care, he won't—"

Gioia felt horror wash over her like a cold fog. "T.J., I don't think you should be telling me all this," she whispered. It was all she could do to keep from grabbing his sleeve and forcing him to tell her everything.

"Thad and I aren't—that is, he hasn't—"

"No? Well, if it's any comfort to you, I think he'll end up telling you a lot more than I have. Just a hunch, you understand?"

The smile he gave her involved more than the set of teeth that were an orthodontist's dream of perfection. It was really rather sweet, and Gioia decided that there might be a bit more to this man than met the eye. And what met the eye would've been enough for most women. To put it bluntly, T.J. Creed was every bit the hunk Edy had said he was.

So why did he leave her completely unmoved? Was she suffering from a hormone deficiency?

Nothing so simple, she was afraid. All her attention, hormones included, were focused on a man who was nowhere near as handsome, nowhere near as suave, and certainly no fashion plate.

None of which made a particle of difference, because handsome or not, he was what she wanted. In all the ways of wanting that mattered. He was tough and tender, stubborn, and as close-mouthed as a clam, but she knew instinctively that underneath that crusty surface of his ran a deep current of passion.

And she wanted that passion for herself. All of it. Not just for a single night, but for a lifetime.

After seeing T.J. off in his showy white sports car, Gioia wandered back into the house. Thad's car was as modest as he was. She was beginning to suspect that might be deliberate. His clothes could charitably be called nondescript, although they were top quality nondescript. Bought for service, not for show. And although he looked tough and fit and entirely masculine wearing them, there was little danger he would ever be mistaken for a male model.

Her head was beginning to ache, and she knew she was going to have to eat something before she got carried away with all this introspection. Self analysis had never been her long suit. She might be a Virgo, and Virgos were supposed to be ever so neat and ready to analyze everything to death, but a friend of John Pirelli's who'd been into that sort of thing had once told her she'd been born with Neptune sitting squarely on her ascendant. Whatever that was. It had sounded pretty soggy, but she hadn't been overly concerned about it. Still, maybe it would account for the totally irrational way she had behaved tonight. She did know that Virgo was one of the earth signs, and Neptune was definitely concerned with water. And water and earth made mud.

"Hockey pucks," she muttered as she dished up a bowl of her neglected chili. She grated cheese over the top, tasted it, and wrinkled her nose. She'd never really cared much for hot Mexican food.

The phone rang just as she was scraping the bottom of her bowl, and she was tempted to let it ring. It was probably Angie again. Or her mother, wanting to warn her not to let Angie off without trying to talk some good common sense into her, which was about as rewarding as trying to teach a rock to swim. There were times when being the eldest of a large family was a royal pain.

"Hello," she said a little too sharply.

"Gioia, this is JoElla Haley. I hope I'm not interrupting anything."

"Oh, hi, JoElla," she said, greeting her friend who lived about a quarter of a mile further out Queen Street. "No, you're not interrupting a thing, I was just getting ready to wash the dishes. How's your foot?"

"The infection's cleared up, and the doctor says I can start driving next week. It'll be a long time before I ever walk barefoot in this room again, I can tell you that. I even had to have a tetanus shot!"

Gioia commiserated with her friend over having stepped on a rusty upholstery tack. "One of these days I'm going to hire you to do something with that wing chair I botched."

"You have to have strong hands and the right kind of machine, for starters. By the way, I've got nine pints of pecans all picked out if you need them. They're in the freezer—same price as always, but that's not why I called. Aren't you working out at the old Timberlake place across the river?"

"Sure am."

"There's a boat works out that way, have you seen it?"

"Pritchard's? I've passed by. It looks like a dump. Don't tell me they're building anything in that old shed."

"I reckon they must be. I got a call from Elmo Pritchard yesterday wanting to know if I could do a set of covers in a hurry. I told him I could get it done in a week's time if I could get right on it, except if they want monograms or anything like that, it'll take longer. The trouble is, I can't get out there to pick up the cushions, and I was wondering..."

"I'll be glad to pick them up for you, and drive you into town to buy fabric. Who do I ask for?"

"That'll get you three free pints of pecans. I really appreciate it, Gioia. The boat's called *Sea Fever*. Just ask for Elmo, and if he's not there, ask for a Mr. Smith."

Seven

Gioia sat on the foot of her bed and dragged the hair-brush dispiritedly through her hair for the twenty-seventh time. It was supposed to be soothing. A hundred strokes every night before bed, and her worries would never follow her into her dreams, according to Granny G.

But then Granny G. had never tried it with her left hand. And Granny G. had never met Thad Creed.

"Twenty-eight, twenty-nine, thirty." She sighed. Her right toes covered her left ones. Another mental security blanket that came from Lord knows where. It was supposed to recirculate her energies or something—or was that touching her thumb with her forefinger?

"Thirty-one, thirty-two, oh, baloney!" She dropped the brush for the third time and just sat there and stared at it. What difference did it make whether or not her hair got a hundred strokes every single night? There was no way she was going to be able to sleep tonight, much less to dream.

All she had to do was close her eyes and he was right there beside her, all six feet of him, crooked nose, stubborn jaw and all.

Thad hunched over the kitchen counter, scribbling notes that were designed to organize his thoughts. After several minutes he crumpled up the paper and scowled at the phone. For two bits he'd call the bastard back and tell him he could pull in the Bureau, the Coast Guard and the Girl Scouts if he thought they could do a better job of finding his damn boat, and if some insurance company wanted to be suckered into paying out an unnecessary claim, that was their lookout, not his!

Okay, so it had taken him a little longer than he'd estimated. This guy was smarter than your average boat thief. But he was beginning to think Summerfield might have a very good reason for not wanting any official noses sniffing too closely at his quarter-of-a-million-dollar toy. She was supposed to have been used strictly for business entertaining, but maybe Summerfield had laid on a few extras in the way of entertainment, and now he was scared witless that a few traces might turn up in a thorough search for hidden identification numbers. The Coast Guard's policy of seizing any boat on which the smallest trace of drugs had been found had brought religion to more than a few boat owners.

Meanwhile, Summerfield was getting antsy and the thief was playing a clever shell game, managing to keep one marina ahead of him and then backtracking in the dead of night. He'd contacted every marina operator and bridge tender between Newport News and Southport, and there was just nowhere else for her to be.

The *Belle Star* or *Starfish* or whatever her current name was, was holed up right under his nose, and meanwhile, he was going in circles. It didn't help matters one damn bit that he couldn't keep his mind on what he was supposed to be doing.

The pencil snapped in his fingers, and Thad swore with soft but deadly efficiency. Gioia Murphy. God, even her name was enough to set him on fire! The last thing he needed now was that kind of a distraction.

Not that he'd ever claimed to be a monk. For a couple of years after he'd gotten out of the hospital, he'd been afraid to risk any bedroom sports. Hell, he figured he was lucky just to be walking!

Then there had been the business of settling his affairs—he'd been offered a desk job with the force, but he wouldn't have lasted a month. Instead, he'd moved into an apartment, rented an office and gotten his private license.

Building a business was another matter. It had taken time, and after a while he'd been glad of an opportunity to relieve the tedium of what was basically a boring job with a little female companionship, which had usually included sex.

But not too often. And lately not at all.

Until last night.

Until last night, in fact, it had been more than a year since he'd met a woman he even wanted to sleep with. And then he'd met Gioia, and he'd been wanting ever since.

At first he'd told himself that she'd be a pleasant interlude, something to keep his senses honed so that he could wind up this job and get on back to Raleigh, but that was before he'd gotten to know her. Now, damn it, he couldn't keep his mind off her for five consecutive minutes. And that was deadly. The guy he was after didn't play for matches. The stakes were high, and anyone who threatened his little venture had better be ready to move fast at a moment's notice.

After tonight, he wouldn't have a prayer. So what next? Tell himself to back off and forget her?

He'd tried that the first time he'd ever seen her. If it hadn't worked then, it didn't stand a snowball's chance now.

It wasn't as if they even had anything in common. Hell, she didn't even know who Don Williams was!

Thad raked aside his notes and ran his fingers through his hair. Okay, so he *knew* what the problem was; what he *didn't* know was how to deal with it. He wasn't the marrying kind, and Gioia definitely wasn't a one-night stand. So what next?

Thirty-five minutes later he pulled up in front of her house and switched off the engine. He'd half expected to see the white Corvette still parked in her driveway. Thank God he wouldn't have to get rid of T.J. first.

Taking a deep, calming breath, he let himself out of the car. It took half a dozen knocks and two blasts of the doorbell to get her attention. He knew damn well she wasn't in bed, because the lights were still on inside.

"Do you always open the door without finding out who's there?" he demanded. *Great. Just what the occasion called for, Creed!*

"If I feel like it. Would you rather I didn't open it at all?"

He rammed his foot in the opening before she could slam it shut. She was standing there barefoot, with a brush in her hand, and her hair was bristling like the hair on a black cat's tail. "You were brushing your hair," he said. *Brilliant. The trained observer at work.*

"You have something against that, too? Speak up. Don't hold anything back. You might get ulcers."

"My, you're sweet tonight." He slipped past her before she could prevent it, and she turned on him, arms crossed over her chest.

"Thank you." Her smile was sugar sweet. "Won't you come in?"

"I thought maybe T.J. might still be here." She wasn't going to invite him to sit down, so he sat anyway. On the sofa.

She took a straight chair that looked as if it might be early Spanish Inquisition. "No, he couldn't stay. Sorry. Did you need him for something? If you hurry, you can probably catch him before he goes out again."

"It's almost eleven."

"I know." That smile again. She wasn't giving an inch.

Moving abruptly, Thad got up and went to stand behind her. She was still holding the hairbrush in her left hand, as if he'd interrupted her in the middle of brushing. And he happened to know she was right-handed.

"Let me do that," he said, his voice rough with the memory of the way all that black silk felt caressing his naked body.

She stiffened, but ignoring her, he removed the brush from her hand and proceeded as if she weren't babbling excuses and trying to get up out of her chair. One hand on her shoulder and one long stroke of the brush was all it took to calm her right down.

He'd have to remember that.

"No one's brushed my hair since I was eight years old," she murmured, arching her neck and leaning away from the chair back.

He lifted a heavy hank in one hand and drew the brush up from underneath. When she shuddered, he closed his eyes and groaned.

"What did you say?" She sounded sleepy, her voice almost slurred. And then she stiffened. "Ouch!"

"What happened? What did I do?" He dropped to his knees beside her, searching her face.

"It's nothing. You just snagged an ear."

"Oh, gee, honey, I'm sorry. Let me see."

But she was turning her head. "No, I . . . it's nothing, honestly. They're a natural hazard. I forgot to warn you to steer around them."

Thad wasn't having any of that. Holding her head against him, he parted her hair and located the injured appendage. It was pretty red. Redder than usual? "Um . . . I think I might have scratched it," he said diffidently.

Gioia tried in vain to retrieve her head, preferably with ears attached, but he refused to let go. "It'll mend. Now, would you please—"

To his astonishment, her whole face was flaming, and it occurred to Thad that she wasn't so much hurt as embarrassed.

"Over these?" he marveled. Without thinking, he leaned forward and took one small lobe between his teeth. At the first stroke of his tongue, she seemed to curl into a small, defensive knot, and he gathered her, knot and all, into his arms. "Hey, now, don't run and hide from me. My ears are twice the size of yours and you don't see me cringing, do you?"

He suckled again for good measure, and nuzzled her neck in the bargain. She was trembling again, and God help him, so was he!

"Gioia? Sweetheart?"

"I'm not your sweetheart," she mumbled against his shoulder.

I wouldn't bet on it, he said silently.

And Gioia was thinking, *Oh, how I wish I were!*

Before she realized what was happening, he stood and swung her up into his arms. Her legs kicked out wildly, and she clutched his shoulders. "Look, this has gone far enough! What happened earlier—well, it was just a fluke. I told you it's not going to happen again."

Ignoring her protests, Thad headed for the stairs.

Gioia began to squirm. "Would you *put me down*?"

"Nope. Be still. If I fall, we both fall."

"Oh, for heaven's sake, Thad, what do you think you're doing?"

"I, uh, well, I'm supposed to be seducing you. At least, that's what I had in mind. You see I had this dream that was so real I could almost taste it. I figured I had to be hallucinating, so I thought I'd check it out. You don't mind, do you?" She buried her face in his neck, and from the way she was shaking, he wasn't certain if she was laughing or crying. "Gioia? Sweetheart? It was a real special kind of dream." And when she still didn't answer—"Hey! Are you okay?"

"Not exactly. Yes. Oh, I don't know!"

"Yeah, me too."

They reached the top of the stairs and she started to laugh aloud. "Thad, I hate to tell you this, but I've moved downstairs."

He shifted her weight, which was beginning to sag a bit, and stared down at her. "The hell you say! When?"

"After you left. After T.J. left. Angie's coming—she doesn't care for an eastern exposure, so I gave her my room."

Manfully, Thad plodded back downstairs, still carrying her in his arms. Gioia thought she heard him mutter something about hardwood floors and kitchen counters, which sounded a bit kinky, but at this point, she would have been willing to try it in the front porch swing.

You're crazy, woman! You're asking for more misery than you're going to be able to handle.

Shut up, idiot—at least he came back didn't he?

The bedroom was chilly and smelled of furniture polish and clean linens, with faint overtones of mothballs. The only light, unfortunately, was a rather grim overhead fixture that cast a distinctly unflattering glare.

Thad lowered her onto the bed and sat down beside her. She could see him flexing his muscles in relief, and it was all she could do not to throw her arms around him right then and there. Bless him, he was as hard as a rock, with the kind of muscles that didn't come from any fancy machine, but as slender as she was, there was a lot of her.

"Thanks for not dropping me," she said, the warmth she felt in her heart spilling over into her voice.

Thad drew his knee up on the bed and gazed down at her. Slowly he reached out and sifted through her hair until he found an ear. "There's not a single part of you that isn't beautiful, Gioia. Don't ever hide yourself."

Her voice unsteady, she said, "While I appreciate the kind words, it was too dark before—you haven't really seen enough of me to form an intelligent opinion."

"A fact I intend to remedy as soon as I can without appearing too greedy." She reached for the switch to turn off the light, but he stayed her hand.

Turning away from the glare, she said, "For instance, my index toes—"

"Your *index toes*?"

"You know what I mean. Anyway, mine come all the way out to the ends of my big toes. You know what that means, don't you?"

"That you're insatiable in bed?"

"That I tend to dominate."

"I can handle that," he said with a whimsical grin that stole the last sliver of common sense right out of her hand.

She had absolutely no defenses when it came to Thaddeus Creed. As if she wanted any. "Thad, why did you come back? Honestly?" she asked softly.

He stared at the lace-edged linen cloth on the oak bedside table for a long moment, and then said, "Because I had to know. Because you've got me to the point where I don't know if I'm coming or going. Because I think I'm in real big trouble, and I wanted to be sure."

She was silent for a moment. "So you came here to seduce me again to find out if you were in trouble? You think that'll help?"

"Oh, well...when you put it that way, it sounds sort of cold-blooded. Except that cold is the last term I'd use to describe the condition of my blood right now. Or any other time when I'm with you. Or even when I'm not, which is getting to be a problem."

"You want to talk about it?"

"Not particularly. Do you?"

Slowly she shook her head. If Thad had needed an invitation, it was there in her eyes, in the way she spread her arms.

He slipped off his shoes first. She was already barefoot. Lifting her to a sitting position, he drew down the covers and then tipped her this way and that while he pulled them under her hips and out of the way.

"You're good at that," she observed, her awareness of him and of what was about to happen increased by astronomical leaps. "Don't tell me you're an ex-nurse, too?"

"My mother's a nurse, but at the moment I'd just as soon leave her out of this." He unbuttoned his shirt and stripped it off, and she could see quite clearly now the distinct pattern of dark hair that formed a *T* on his chest and disappeared under his belt. There were two small round scars on his right shoulder, and Gioia flinched, torn between wanting to ask and not wanting to know. Somewhere along the line, his pain had become her pain, his joy hers.

With trembling fingers, she pulled at the bottom of her own shirt and started to lift it when his hand came down over hers. "Let me," he said deeply. "I didn't want you to get cold first."

"C-cold? Hardly," she whispered, mesmerized as he removed her shirt, efficiently eased her jeans over her hips and stared down at her, his eyes glowing with need and something more.

She had changed into her work clothes the minute she'd gotten rid of T.J., and now she almost regretted it. The bathrobe would have been quicker.

While she was still struggling to manage the elaborate business of breathing, he released his own belt. She heard the dry rasp of a zipper and tried in vain to turn her head away. Or at least avert her eyes. Oh, Lord, she'd lost all sense of modesty as well as every shred of common sense! It was even worse than before.

If Gioia had harbored one last, lingering doubt, it disappeared like a wisp of fog under the tender assault of Thad's kiss. His lips caressed, they teased, they taunted. His tongue tantalized as it explored, advancing and retreating, gently at first, and then boldly, rapidly, until she was frantic with need.

Nor were his hands idle all this time. They searched out the familiar contours of her body, the small slopes of her breasts with their aroused and elongated peaks, the sudden dip of her waist and the sweeping flow of her hips. He spanned her flat abdomen with one hand, sliding it from side to side and then downward until she was moaning softly in the back of her throat.

"Oh, please. Oh, Thad!"

"Shhh, patience, love. I haven't even got to those dominant toes of yours yet."

And he proceeded to do so, after first kissing his way down her leg, with forays along the way that rendered her incapable of anything beyond the occasional feeble whisper.

Feeling much bolder this time, Gioia wanted to explore, too. That broad, tantalizing thatch of fur she'd glimpsed on his chest, the muscular thigh that could lock around her and hold her a willing captive forever.

"I need to touch you, too," she pleaded once, and he moved up her heated body slowly, dropping nibbling kisses in the crease of her thighs, her tiny navel and the shallow valley of her breasts.

Then, obediently, he rolled over on his back beside her, his chest rising and falling rapidly as he labored to control his breathing. He was making himself totally vulnerable to her, and Gioia, even as she tentatively began to explore his rugged masculine body, knew that this was something he rarely did. For any woman.

It gave her a small measure of hope, and she rested her head on the flat plane below his massive rib-cage and closed her hand gently around his manhood.

A shudder racked his body, and she lifted her head, fearing she had somehow hurt him. "Was I—did I—?"

His hand closed over hers, and he showed her how to caress him, but a moment later, he groaned and removed her hand, bringing it up to his lips.

"Sweetheart, I'm only human. Let me..."

And he did. Until she was writhing helplessly, no part of her body unkissed, unloved. Again and again he brought her to the edge of sanity, always holding back until she could bear no more.

He turned away for a moment, and she drew a deep, shuddering breath, and then he was back. Over her. His face flushed and his eyes glittering, he stared down at her as if he were memorizing her face.

I love you. Please... Hovering dangerously near the rim, Gioia could feel him against her, and she lifted her hips. Thad lowered himself until, for a single instant, she bore his whole body weight. Her arms went around him and she wrapped her legs around his hips, holding him to her with all her strength.

She felt branded—as if his full weight had somehow impressed itself indelibly on her soul.

And then he came into her, and suddenly they were caught up in the whirlwind. "Ah, sweet Joy," he cried just before they were swept away in a state of pure bliss.

Gioia didn't know how long she slept the first time. Sometime during the night she awoke with her head on Thad's shoulder, and fearing for his circulation, she eased away. He murmured something in his sleep and turned over onto his side, drawing her back against his front.

Once again she awakened, this time to find him tickling her arm with the tips of his fingers ever so lightly. "You awake?" he whispered.

"No," she replied.

"Good. I wouldn't want to disturb you," he said, and then he proceeded to make love to her again until tears streamed down her cheeks.

"God, you're not crying, are you, darling?" He had pulled her down on top of him in the sweet lingering afterglow.

"Uh-uh." She grabbed a corner of quilt and mopped her eyes. "I get emotional sometimes. I cry when I watch marching bands, too. It doesn't mean anything."

They slept, exhausted, and when she woke up the next time there was a watery gray light filtering through the sheer white curtains. She'd known even before she'd opened her eyes that the sky would be cloudy.

Just as she'd known the pillow next to her own would be empty. Her clothes had been picked up and neatly draped over the chair, her hairbrush lying on top.

Thad's clothes were gone. As was he. There was no note. Neither of them had said anything about later—tonight. Tomorrow. But he'd left her a full pot of coffee, hot, rich and fragrant to wake up to.

Which was better than nothing, but not a whole lot better.

Eight

A few days ago there had been only two masts visible above the roof of the boat shed. Now there were three. And one of them was the *Belle Star*. He had no proof—not yet. It was only a gut feeling, but Thad had learned over a lot of years to trust his instincts. The biggest mistakes of his life had been made when he'd gone against them.

From his position on the Pasquotank side of the river near Knobbs Creek, he could look almost directly across to the Camden side and see the boat shed quite clearly. From the outside. There was only one way to see inside the place, and he was beginning to think he was going to have to risk it.

The hunter-with-lost-dog ploy was out. He'd already used it twice, and been assured by the fellow who owned the place that there had been no dogs, lost or otherwise, anywhere near there.

He could break out his yachting togs, which were probably pretty wrinkled by now, and ask to inspect the premises with a view to keeping a boat there. But if he were recognized, he'd be back at the starting gate. Blackbeard, as he'd dubbed his modern-day pirate, had a sixth sense that told him when the chase was getting too close.

Damn it, all he needed was one good look inside that boat shed, and then, if the *Belle Star* was there, he'd have to work out a way to get aboard her. There *had* to be some way! The trouble was, Blackbeard was onto every trick. He'd probably used most of them to lure unsuspecting crew members and owners off their boats in the first place.

Two hundred years ago Thad might have fired a shot across her bow and boarded her at gunpoint to search for evidence. Today a bit more finesse was required.

For better or worse, he still tended to think like a cop. Damn it, if he had a court order, he could search her for proof. The trouble was, he couldn't get a court order without showing probable cause, and he couldn't show probable cause without some sort of proof. Catch-22.

This guy would be convincing, too. He'd have a brand-new title and registration in his hip pocket before he ever cleared port that first time. Within minutes the ketch would have been given a new name, had fresh paint slapped on here and there for color, and for all he knew, a slew of family photographs screwed to the bulkhead of the master cabin.

The guy was good. He was smart, and unlike a few of the hopheads who tried piracy, he could easily pass for the owner of a quarter of a million dollars worth of teak, fiberglass and state-of-the-art electronics. According to the security guards at one of the marinas where Thad had come within half a day of catching up with him, he was passing himself off as Alexander Workman-Smith, a retired stockbroker, mid-fifties, average height, gray hair, dark, neatly trimmed beard. Which might or might not be real. He was reputed to be a quiet guy with a taste for pastel deck shoes and expensive jewelry.

He could afford it. According to what Thad had been able to dig up so far, he'd gotten away with close to four million dollars worth of merchandise over the past few years. Place your order and he'd deliver, Sail or power, it didn't seem to make a difference. Nor did the odd body that got in the way. Two dock guards at a club near St. Augustine had been wasted when they'd gotten a little too nosy, and there was no doubt in Thad's mind as to who was responsible. Insurance companies were screaming their heads off, the Bureau was itching to get involved, but unless Summerfield called them in, their hands were tied. And if they came in on it, Thad was out. And with him, his rep as a P.I. who could deliver.

No way was he going to let that happen! The Bureau had equipment that could take a flake of dandruff and tell you what a suspect had eaten for breakfast. The Creed agency was small, but it was gaining a pretty solid reputation, even if it was headed up by a poor slob who spent most of his time crawling around on his hands and knees in a stinking mud hole.

Half an hour later Thad crossed the bridge into Camden County and headed for Riverton Road. The seat of his pants was wet, his feet were numb and he stank like a polecat from slogging through acres of black slimy gunk. God knows how many creatures had sacrificed themselves to produce such a smell. He'd give his wisdom teeth and half his Don Williams collection to be transported to somewhere warm and dry. Preferably to an orange house on a country road outside Riverton. Preferably to a bed in that same house.

And preferably not alone.

Hell, as long as he was dreaming, he might as well make a good job of it. Put a woman in his arms—not just any woman, but one with eyes like five-carat sapphires, hair like the inside of midnight and a body that could make the dead rise up and walk. Put a pot of something thick and meaty on the back burner, a pan of corn bread in the oven, something slow and sexy on the stereo and turn off all but one dim light.

There was only one problem with that picture: him. He didn't fit. T.J. was more her speed, and by now she'd probably realized that. After last night...

God, after last night! He'd been out off his rocker to go back there, not just once, but twice! She'd been so sweet, so giving, so wonderful in her own prickly way. He'd suspected before he'd even fallen asleep the first time that he was in deep trouble. After the second time, he'd known for sure. Once he'd awakened and propped himself on his elbow to watch her sleep. The feeling of sadness that had come over him was like nothing he'd ever experienced.

The hell he'd gone through when Jackie had walked out on him had been nothing to compare with the feeling of loss, of deprivation, that had suddenly stricken him last night. Eight years ago he'd been groggy from painkillers and too involved in the business of having his backside damn near shot off by that son of a bitch cop killer's woman to worry about a little thing like a wife who didn't particularly cotton to the notion of being married to a cripple. And when he'd finally left the hospital, limping like a three-legged dog and about thirty pounds under par, he hadn't wanted her back.

That had been trouble. But this was *trouble*! If he couldn't even hang on to a woman like Jackie, God knows he didn't have a prayer with a woman like Gioia Murphy.

* * *

After one look at the rutted track that led down to the boat works, Gioia parked up near the road and continued the journey on foot. There were boat trailers everywhere, some new, some rusted and falling apart. Old drums, spools of cable, scraps of colorful rope and a makeshift crane were scattered around like children's toys. Two tall pines had been left standing, one of them dead, the other barely living. A crossbar had been nailed between them, and what looked like the engine of a car was suspended from it by a rusted cable.

Except for a brier-covered trash dump that leaned against a back corner of the vast old metal building, catching dead leaves and any other bits of debris the wind carried past, the place was barren. Evidently Pritchard's Boat Yard wasn't really big on landscaping.

The door was ajar, but there was no one in evidence. "Elmo?" she called out. "Anyone?"

The sound of hammering came from one of the sheltered sailboats bobbing gently on the water. "Elmo? Mr. Smith?"

"What d'you want? Elmo's not here."

A man came out from behind the boat on the far end. Even in filthy coveralls he was fairly nice-looking, in a mature way. He was hardly the type she would have expected to find in a junkyard like this, but then what did she know about boat yards? Maybe they were like garages. Sometimes the best mechanics were to be found in the rattiest-looking places.

"I came for some cushions...that need to be covered? JoElla Haley asked me to pick them up for her. She said if Elmo wasn't here, a Mr. Smith would know about them."

The man stared at her for so long that she began to wonder if she had varnish on her nose, but then he turned and indicated the boat he'd been working on. "I'm Smith. Come on, I'll get them for you." He was wearing a pair of filthy coveralls, but his deck shoes looked like the expensive kind, and she'd bet a nickel that the ring on his little finger was no zircon. At first glance she'd taken him for a caretaker. Now she wasn't so sure.

"Wow, that's a bunch of cushions," she said after he'd brought up an armload. "Is this the lot?"

"There are eight more, all larger."

"I guess they'll squash down. I've got a pretty big car."

"Where you parked?"

"Up near the road. I was afraid of picking up a nail. I just had to buy a new tire recently and this place . . ." She shook her head. "On the other hand, I don't look forward to walking all the way out to the road half a dozen times. I don't suppose they're heavy, but they look pretty awkward to carry."

"Never mind. I'll get a handcart."

"Oh, great! Shall I get the rest of the cushions?"

"They're just inside, stacked on a locker." He indicated the sleek vessel on the end.

"It's . . . she's a lovely boat."

He didn't bother to reply. So much for doing someone a favor.

Gioia stepped aboard gingerly and ducked into the only opening she saw. The woodwork was beautiful, and she wished she could stay to examine it, but Scrooge didn't look as if he would welcome her interest. The cushions had already been stripped of their old covers, and she shoved them through the door, which was probably called something nautical. She could imagine Mr. Smith's derision if she called a door a door or a window a window on his fancy boat.

Make that yacht. The *Sea Fever* was definitely no mere "boat." She'd have loved the grand tour, never having been on anything more luxurious than the Ocracoke-Cedar Island ferry. "Fat chance," she murmured, taking one last look around.

It was then that she glimpsed the corner of a cushion that had slipped down between a chest of some sort and a clever folding table. Had Mr. Smith missed it? It would have been easy to do. If she hadn't seen the flash of color, she'd have missed it, too.

Tugging it out, she examined it, wondering if she should take it along with the rest. On the other hand, the cover looked almost new. Dark green, of an expensive-looking material, it was neatly corded on the edges. The name *Belle Star*, centered by an anchor, had been embroidered in the same bottle-green in the lower right-hand corner. Subtle, she thought. Tasteful.

Only the name was wrong, of course. Perhaps his last boat had been the *Belle Star*, and this was a keepsake. More likely, it had blown off another yacht, and he'd only picked it up.

At any rate, it had nothing to do with her. If he'd wanted it covered, he would have said so. Mr. Smith didn't strike her as the sort of man who overlooked the least detail, not even one small cushion.

After a last look over her shoulder, Gioia stepped out onto the sagging wharf. "Bloody swank," she murmured, picking up four of the foam cushions and heading for her car. On the way she passed Smith, who had located a handcart.

"I'll carry these if you can stack the rest on the cart. They're going to look great, you know. JoElla does wonderful work. What color are you having them done over in?"

He sent her a frostbitten look. "Mrs. Haley has instructions."

Well, la-de-da! So much for making conversation, too. She stalked off ahead, barely able to see over her burden, while Smith struggled to negotiate the rutted track with the heavy-duty handcart. Unlocking the trunk, she carefully placed the largest cushion over the stain where the varnish had spilled out on the carpeting. If Prince Charming, with his yellow suede deck shoes, his pinky ring and his stingy little beard, was worried about keeping his precious cushions clean, he should have left the old covers on. JoElla might have been able to reuse the zippers, but his sort wouldn't worry over something so trivial.

Gioia unlocked her car and helped stuff the rest of the load into the back seat, and then she climbed in. "Well...goodbye, Mr. Smith. You'll be pleased with these when JoElla gets them done, I promise you. They'll be prettier than ever."

Okay, she'd tried. But her efforts were completely ignored by the man who stood scowling at her rear bumper and massaging his jaw. So maybe he had a toothache. Did that mean he couldn't even manage a civil word?

Gioia slammed the door, and without a backward glance, drove off. "Thanks for the gigantic favor, Miss Murphy," she muttered under her breath as she kicked up a cloud of dust on the unpaved road. Not that she'd done it for him. Imagine owning such a lovely boat and being such a miserable jerk. Some people didn't know when they were well off.

By the time she was halfway home, the clouds had covered the setting sun. Gioia took off her sunglasses and laid them on the dash. One of these days she was going to get herself a pair of pink ones for days like this. She loved gray days, but not if she had to go out in them. Gray days were

for staying home and cooking soup, for munching pop-
corn and listening to *Pathétique*, or reading a three-hanky
romance with a sentimental, happy-ever-after ending.

Forget the pink glasses. What she needed was a vacation! Or a full-time lover. Living alone had its advantages—at least she didn't have to take a number and wait
for the bathroom any longer. And talking to plants and
fish was okay, too, unless you happened to be in the mood
for a nice juicy argument.

But sometimes lying in bed, staring at the ceiling, she
couldn't help but wonder if that was all she could expect.
Every time she thought she'd found someone something
happened. Usually Angie, bless her. She'd begun to
hope—that is, after last night she'd sort of thought that
Thad...

But then he'd left—twice—without a word about seeing
her again, and he hadn't called this morning. She'd stayed
at home as long as she could, but then she'd told herself
she wasn't going to put her whole life on hold just because one man—one *wonderful* man—a man with whom
she happened to be in love...

All right, so she hadn't exactly expected a commitment
from him. After all, they'd both wanted what had happened. But he could have left a note. Or called her this
morning to say hello, or to tell her...

Oh, hell, just to say *anything*! Just to let her know that
last night had meant something to him, too. And now,
even if he did come back, Angie would be here, and
everything would be different.

"I thought you weren't ever coming home," Angie
complained before Gioia could even remove her vest and
cap. "You drove right past. I thought maybe you'd
changed your mind about having me."

She embraced her younger sister, automatically bending over to exchange kisses. "Oh, honey, I'm so glad to see you. It's been ages! I had to drop off some cushions at my neighbor's house first. She does upholstery and custom work for a lot of boat yards around here. Her husband died last year, leaving her a mortgage, a worn-out pecan grove, a monster sewing machine and a five-year-old son."

"Don't you even want to know what happened?"

"I just told you." Gioia heel-toed her rubber moccasins and stepped out of them. "His tractor turned over, and—oh, you mean what happened to *you*."

"Of course I mean me! Who did you think I meant?"

For the next hour or so, while Gioia changed out of her work clothes, showered and put together supper for both of them, she heard more than she really cared to know about Jack Loggins, M.D., who was really the sweetest man, and whose wife really didn't understand him.

"Honestly, Angie, you didn't fall for that old line, did you?"

"What old line? I didn't fall for anything. I was only trying to cheer him up. His poor ego needed stroking because that wife of his is a real harpy. Sometimes I don't even think she likes him! She refuses to have any children because it would interfere with getting her doctorate in something nobody ever heard of."

"Angie, is all this really necessary?" Gioia's hand was hurting, and she couldn't prevent her mind from straying to her own problems. Correction. Thad was a problem, all right; the only thing he wasn't, was hers.

The look in her sister's eyes made her feel like a real heel.

"Well, I don't suppose it's very interesting to someone independent like you, who has her own life and her own house and all that, but for me it was just awful! I mean, honestly, Joy, you should have heard the awful things she said to me. You'd have thought I was having an affair with her precious husband or something, to hear her go on.''

''Were you?''

Angie's eyes threatened to overflow, but never quite did. ''No, I wasn't. We were friends, that's all. We got along great, and I stayed late a few nights when he needed to talk, but he never even kissed me, Joy, honestly.''

Gioia had to believe her. Angie was no liar. The trouble was that she'd never fully understood the effect she had on men. Once they got over the initial shock of seeing her, they were determined to have her. And when they discovered that she was a genuinely sweet and caring person, they wanted to take care of her, and after that it was only a matter of time until they were total basket cases. ''I believe you, honey. Now, aren't you about ready for bed? You had a pretty long drive.''

''It's barely eight o'clock,'' the tiny blonde wailed. ''What do you do around here for fun? Don't you have any friends?''

''Well...sure. There's Mack and Edy Canfield, and JoElla...''

''I mean single friends—men. Haven't you found a boyfriend yet?''

Gioia had to smile. The years hadn't changed her sister much. Tact had never been her strong suit, but she'd never been malicious. There wasn't a mean bone in her exquisite little body. She was simply...Angelica. And if Gioia could have produced a man out of her hat—any man, just so long as he was presentable enough to distract poor Angie from her troubles—she would have done it.

There was only Thad, and that was out of the question now. Besides, he and Angie would never hit it off. Angie was just too—

And Thad. He was entirely too—

Absently Gioia rubbed the top of her left foot with her right one. Well, they just wouldn't, that was all.

"Actually, I did meet someone recently," she began, and Angie leaned forward, her eyes glistening like wet aquamarines.

"Who? Is he nice? Is he good-looking?" Her small face fell. "Are you interested in him, Joy? Because if you are, maybe it would be better if—"

"If he didn't meet you," Gioia finished. She smiled. "Listen, kitten, if I were seriously interested in a man, I wouldn't let you get within a hundred miles of him, but T.J.'s not my type. And I'm definitely not his."

"Then couldn't you just sort of invite him over for coffee or something? If I had something to take my mind off all the awful things Cassie Loggins said to me, right in the middle of the public library on a Saturday afternoon, where everybody could hear her, I'd probably sleep a lot better tonight."

"Lordy, honey, you don't ask for much, do you? The only time I ever called a man and invited him over, he was a plumber and I was ankle-deep in water. Even then he didn't come until the next afternoon. Besides, T.J.'s probably out on a date."

"Then it wouldn't hurt to call, would it? Because if he's not home, he'll never know."

No, but someone else might, Gioia told herself, and she'd die before she would call Thad Creed and ask him for anything. "I don't know, Angie..."

"I should have gone to visit Aunt Jane. At least she doesn't start yawning right after supper and go to bed with a book before the news is even over."

"So why didn't you?" asked Gioia, none too flattered by the comparison.

"She'd fuss over me and say it was probably my fault, and honestly, Joy, it wasn't."

"I know, honey. It's never been your fault." Thad had stared at her picture long enough. If he ever got a look at the genuine article, he'd be just as gone as the rest of them. Including Angie's boss. Angie might think their relationship had been all perfectly innocent, but that didn't mean the harpy had been barking up the wrong tree. Doctor or no doctor, Loggins was a man, wasn't he?

"There's a pretty good movie on TV tonight," she said in a tactful effort to change the subject. "It's not a rerun, either."

"Do you get cable?"

"Sorry. It doesn't stretch this far out."

In the middle of Angie's sigh, someone began pounding on the front door. Gioia felt her breath catch in the middle of her chest. She would have known that pounding anywhere. Never a polite tap, tonight it practically rattled the windowpanes.

She actually had her hand on the doorknob when the door was flung back, barely missing her nose. "Do come in," she drawled, eyes snapping with anger at his unnecessary forcefulness. "Just like on TV, isn't it? Do policemen ever wait to be invited inside?"

Thad took all of three steps before he stopped to glare at her, his eyes missing nothing of her freshly shampooed hair, her oldest, softest pair of jeans and the ivory turtleneck top she'd pulled on hurriedly, not bothering to wear anything under it. "At least you're not lying in a ditch somewhere with your throat slit!"

Her jaw fell open. If he'd pulled out a gun and started shooting out the lights, she couldn't have been more stunned. "Wh-what?"

She sniffed the air for any trace of alcohol. That wasn't the statement of a rational man, drunk or sober. And Thad appeared to be stone-cold sober. Alarmingly so. He looked more like a soldier of fortune than an ex-policeman, insurance salesman or whatever he was, who was currently visiting his brother. Dressed in canvas pants, a black pullover and muddy hunting boots, he was either blushing or badly windburned, or both. As for his eyes, they were burning holes right through to the back of her head.

"I don't know what your particular problem is, but if you can't control your temper any better than that, you can just damn well take it and...and go jump! And shut the door when you leave!" Arms crossed over her chest, she was shaking like a leaf, and that made her even angrier. How *could* he! Was this the man who had laughed with her and loved with her until she'd lost all hope of redemption?

In a pig's eye!

Gioia was only dimly aware that Angie had pushed herself between them and was glaring up at Thad. He ignored her as if she were less than a bothersome fly. "I need to talk to you. Alone," he added pointedly.

He could act the barbarian all he wanted too—she refused to sink to his level. "Angie, this...*creature* is Thaddeus Creed. His brother is the lovely man I was telling you about. Mr. Creed, this is my sister, Angelica."

"I'm sure she'll excuse us, won't you, Miss—uh...?" His eyes never left Gioia's face. She could actually feel them paring away the flesh from her bones.

She took a deep breath. The sooner he spoke his piece, the sooner he would leave. And the sooner he left, the sooner she could start throwing things and screaming. Which should help a whole lot! "All right then, say what you have to say and then get out."

"Alone." He spoke through clenched teeth, his lips barely moving.

And then Angie jabbed a finger into his chest. "Whatever you have to say to my sister, you can say in front of me! We don't have any secrets."

For a pint-size blonde wearing a periwinkle sweater dress with lace collar and cuffs, she looked surprisingly militant. But then the Murphys had always gone to bat for one another. As some of them were inclined to be rather hotheaded, they'd all had a lot of practice.

"This doesn't concern you," Thad growled.

"Oh, yes, it does!"

"Oh, for pity's sake!" Gioia was within an inch of walking out on the pair of them. "Look, I haven't the foggiest idea what this is all about, but between the two of you I've had it up to here!"

The response was instantaneous. Angie stepped back with the same wounded look on her face that had had grown men groveling since she was fourteen. "Well, excuse me for caring!" she said, flouncing off to sulk all alone on the sofa under the pink-shaded floor lamp.

As for Thad, he seemed to be making some sort of effort to control his temper, albeit an unsuccessful one. He began pacing. As both his boots and his pants were caked with mud that was just beginning to dry, he left a trail of gray dirt behind him.

Gioia refused to break the brittle silence. Whatever his problem was, he had no business taking it out on her. Any minute now he was going to do a double take and realize just who had jabbed him in the chest, and then Gioia could have the pleasure of sitting back and watching her little sister drain the steam out of his boiler.

She'd slit her own throat first! What the devil had he been raving about—her lying somewhere in a ditch? "Do you want to tell me what your problem is?'' Damn it, even in filthy hunting clothes, which had to be the unsexiest garb devised by mankind, he looked a hundred and fifty percent male.

He scowled at her. "It's not my problem. It's yours."

She lifted both eyebrows at that. "My problem! You come in here as mad as a bull, ranting about—"

"I wasn't ranting, and I certainly wasn't mad!" he shot back. Angie's head was bouncing back and forth, like a spectator at a tennis match.

"Oh, no? I'd like to know what the dickens you call it!"

"Common concern!"

"Concern! Good Lord, if that's the way you show concern, heaven help anyone who makes you mad!"

"Look, I told you we need to talk, but—isn't there somewhere we could go?"

"I'm not going anywhere with a man who barges into my house and threatens to slit my—"

"I did not threaten you!" Thad roared.

He'd come to stand over her, smelling of cold December night air, of wet marshes, of warm healthy male. It was an unexpectedly intoxicating mixture, and Gioia's pulses tripped into double time. She stepped back, and finding herself backed up against the wing chair, sat down rather suddenly.

Thad leaned over her, bracing himself on the chair arms. He was so close she could see the tiny scar on the left side of his chin, and the deep grooves that bracketed his mouth. "Look, uh, maybe your sister would like to drive over across the bridge and take in a movie."

"She just got into town. She doesn't even know her way around."

"Well, doesn't she have any friends here? Hasn't she ever visited you here before?"

"No, she doesn't, and no, she hasn't."

And then Angie spoke up, her voice as guileless as if she were totally unaware of the tension that shimmered between the other two present. "Joy was about to call your brother. She thought he might like to come over for coffee or something. Do you happen to know if he's home?"

"Angelica? Please be quiet."

It was Thad who took over at that point. He looked at Angie as if he were really seeing her for the first time, and Gioia could almost feel herself crawling into a small, protective shell. "No, she's right. I was rude to barge in on your first night, but, look, I'm sorry, Angelica, okay? Let me give T.J. a ring and see if he's still there."

Nine

To fill the awkward interval, Gioia had suggested coffee, hoping for a moment alone to regain some sort of composure. But first Thad and then Angie had followed her, and now they sat around the kitchen table, nursing mugs of freshly brewed coffee and making small talk.

Meanwhile, Gioia was no closer to composure than she'd been when Thad had hurtled into her house in a flaming temper, accusing her of some nameless crime, and then refusing to elaborate.

At least his temper seemed to have cooled off. Funny— she would never have thought he'd be the type to fly off the handle that way.

But then she'd been wrong about something else, too. She'd taken it for granted that after one good look at Angie, he'd be as besotted as any other man with eyes in his head. So far he'd paid the ex-Miss Guilford County, twice Homecoming Queen and winner of four Beautiful Baby

Contests, about as much attention as he'd paid the supper dishes that were piled in the sink.

"I don't believe Gioia mentioned what it is that you do, Thad," Angie said, her voice just a little bit softer, a little more Southern.

Thad looked at her as if he couldn't quite remember who she was. "I, uh, I'm in research," he told her, turning back to Gioia before the words were even out. "Sorry about all the mud. My car got stuck, and I had a hell of a time getting it unstuck, and then I was in such a hurry, I didn't want to waste any more time. If you think I'm a mess, you ought to see the Ford."

Research? This was the first Gioia had heard about any research. Was that what had taken him from a beach in the West Indies to whatever or wherever else T.J. had mentioned? Before she could ask, the doorbell sounded "Shave and a Haircut, Two Bits," and Thad shoved back his chair and stood, a look of relief on his rugged features. "That'll be T.J. I'll get it."

The minute he left the room, Angie leaned across the table. "Research? What kind of research? Is it something to do with all this oil drilling business they keep talking about in the news? They're called roughnecks, you know, the men who work on those things. He sort of looks like a roughneck, doesn't he? Honestly, Joy, you could do better than that."

"Better than what? There's nothing between us," Gioia lied through her teeth. If she'd had her hopes for a few hours, they were rapidly slipping away. She would never have thought a man who could be so tender could turn around and treat her as if she'd done something heinous.

"Come on, I'm your sister. I saw how you looked at him. You were looking at his body, too, Joy."

"I was not!"

"Were, too." A teasing smile produced a pair of perfectly matched pair of dimples in Angie's cheeks.

Gioia stared at the doorway through which Thad had disappeared. She could hear the low murmur of male voices from the living room, but no matter how hard she tried she couldn't make out a word. Something was going on here and she had a right to know what it was. Furthermore, she was going to demand that he tell her precisely what he was up to, why he was being so secretive and what, if anything, his intentions were.

Scratch that last. She had a strong feeling she wouldn't like what he told her. But then, knowing him, he wouldn't tell her anything, anyway.

"Please don't be mad with me, Joy. I was only teasing."

Angie's soft voice broke through Gioia's thoughts, and she realized she'd been scowling at the sugar bowl.

"Oh, golly, you haven't gone and fallen in love with him, have you?"

Gioia shifted the scowl to the woman seated across from her. "Don't be ridiculous. Of course I'm not in love! We're... friends, that's all. Hardly even that."

"He didn't sound all that friendly when he barged in here. I thought he was going to explode or something."

"That's just Thad's way." Gioia was mildly disgusted to hear herself defending the man she'd been ready to clobber five minutes ago. "He has a... He has this... Well, he's sort of—"

"A clod," Angie finished for her. "I mean, those clothes! He looks like one of those old western types who live nine hundred miles from anywhere. Does he talk to his horse and eat beans out of a tin can?"

Gioia bristled. "Just because he doesn't spend half his time primping in front of a mirror, that doesn't mean he doesn't know how to dress when the occasion demands it. Besides, I happen to think he looks incredibly sexy in boots, a black pullover and a pair of nicely fitted hunting pants.''

"Sexy! The difference between you and me is—"

"Is the difference between an adult and a perennial adolescent," Gioia snapped.

"Huh! Well, since neither one of *you* two is getting any younger, I guess that means I'm the adolescent." Angie had just settled in for another good sulk when the men appeared in the doorway.

At any other time it would have been funny, watching the reaction of two physically superlative specimens confronting each other for the first time. T.J. couldn't have looked more stunned if he'd walked into a plate-glass window.

As for Angie, she stared up at the golden Adonis—tonight he was dressed all in white, in December yet, with white flannels, white turtleneck and an off-white cable-knit pullover. Gioia decided he looked like a model in a gin and tonic ad.

Angie's eyes widened. Her chest lifted and swelled as she drew in a deep breath, and then her lashes went to work. Gioia could practically feel the draft from where she sat.

Someone made introductions—afterwards, Gioia was never sure which of them had done it. T.J., his voice sounding at least an octave deeper than she remembered, said, "I couldn't help but notice when I was coming over the bridge how lovely all the lights from Riverside Drive look reflected across the water. Some of the yachts are already decorated for Christmas. The reflections look like strings of emeralds, rubies and diamonds tossed out across a bed of black velvet.''

Gioia sneaked a peek at Thad to see if he was going to laugh or throw up. Surely not even Angie could swallow that one with a straight face.

"Oh, it sounds just heavenly," Angie said breathlessly. "We don't have anything like that in Silasville. All we have is little ol' Weavers Creek, and that's almost always muddy."

They wafted out, with T.J. first helping Angie with her white mohair coat, taking forever to lift her hair outside the collar. They were holding hands before they got to the foot of the walk.

"Did you catch a whiff of something in the air just now?" Gioia asked when they'd gone.

"You mean smoke, or overripe baloney?" Thad's lips twitched once or twice. It wasn't exactly a smile, but it was the next best thing.

"You know what else I noticed? They look alike."

He nodded thoughtfully. "The coloring mostly. They could easily pass for brother and sister."

"Somehow I have a feeling they won't."

This time he did smile. It was a grin, in fact. "Somehow I have a feeling you're right. Do you mind?"

"Do you?" she asked cautiously. She still couldn't quite credit the fact that Thad had met Angie and called in his brother to take her off his hands.

And then her own smile faded as she remembered why he was there. "Thad, why *are* you here, anyway?"

"Yeah," he growled, twisting the mug in his hands. Now that the moment of truth had arrived, he wasn't sure how to go about broaching the subject. After scaring the hell out of her, it was a bit late to be inquiring politely after her health, particularly since he'd promised himself to stay away until he got his head sorted out.

Thad had always operated on a need-to-know basis. Gioia didn't need to know any more than it took to make her stay the hell away from Pritchard's Boat Yard.

How well did she know Smith? Did he know where she lived? Thad couldn't believe she was mixed up in this business. She wasn't the type, and anyway, it didn't make sense. The guy worked alone. He had a reputation for keeping outside contacts to an absolute minimum, and when the occasion demanded he could be very effective in cutting his risks.

God, when he'd seen her huddled over something in the back seat of her car with that creep, he'd almost driven into a ditch! Instead, he'd driven on past until he'd found a place to stash his car where it couldn't be seen from the road. Then he'd crept as close as he'd dared.

By the time he'd gotten there, she was just driving off. Smith had turned away, but then—and this was what had made his blood turn to ice water—he'd turned back and watched her out of sight. And then he'd taken a piece of paper out of his pocket and written something on it. Her licence number, more than likely.

"This is going to sound kind of strange, but humor me, will you?" Thad drew in a deep breath and launched into a rough sketch of how he'd followed the trail of a stolen ketch to Pritchard's Boat Yard.

"I thought you sold insurance. T.J. said something about a man calling you about insurance, didn't he?"

And then he had to explain about Summerfield, and his threat to strike a deal with his insurance company unless Thad came up with something concrete in a short time. Summerfield needed money. Rather badly, from the sound of things. Evidently he wasn't averse to making a false claim—or in this case, a premature claim. And if the insurance investigator had to start all over again at ground zero, he just might win out.

"Uh, actually, I'm more like an investigator," he said almost apologetically.

Gioia took a moment to digest the revelation. "You mean like Thomas Magnum, P.I.?"

His eyes crinkled, and he grinned at the empty coffee mug. "Not exactly. The Creed Agency is pretty small—no fancy electronic labs. Not even a revolver and a bottle of rye in the bottom of a filing cabinet. A few years ago I happened to get lucky on a case involving a boatload of smuggled pre-Columbian artifacts. That led to a stolen boat claim, and that led to a few more. I, uh, sort of got this reputation as a finder of stolen yachts. And the crazy thing is, I get sick as a dog on anything bigger than a rowboat."

Gioia got up and poured him more coffee. Without asking, she scooped up a bowl of the chili Angie had turned up her nose at and popped it into the microwave. From the look of him, he hadn't taken time to eat. "Do you like cheese on your chili?" she asked him, and then tried to interpret the look he gave her. It was only leftover chili she was offering him, not a five-course dinner with herself thrown in for dessert. Not again. She wasn't *that* crazy.

"Chili? Homemade? The real stuff? If you say you've got a pan of corn bread in the oven, I'll know I'm at home in bed in the middle of the best dream I ever had."

"Sorry to wake you up, but the best I can do is saltines. The chili's homemade, all right, but I don't make it very often. I'm afraid it might be a little hot."

Thad took one taste and got up to rummage among her condiments. "No Texas Pete?"

"Sorry. There's black pepper. You must have an asbestos gullet."

He finished two bowls of chili and half a tube of saltines, then drank the last of the coffee. Afterward, he insisted on doing all the dishes for her.

"You've got no business getting that hand wet," he reminded her.

Gioia leaned her hips against the kitchen table and watched in open appreciation while he dealt with the mess she'd left in her sink. She hated doing dishes. Somehow she'd always seemed to end up with that chore when she was growing up. Besides, it was a lot more fun to watch Thad's muscular, hairy forearms trailing soapsuds from one side of the sink to the other. The pink-and-white-checked towel jammed into his belt didn't detract one iota from his masculinity.

"Funny, isn't it," she murmured, leaning back on her hands. "You come in here roaring like a lion and end up washing dishes like a lamb."

"I've never seen a dishwashing lamb. But then I never spent much time in the country."

"Where did you spend your time?" She held her breath, certain he would put her off with some joking remark, or a question of his own.

Thad rinsed the last glass and turned it upside down on the dish rack. He dried his hands on the towel, then dropped it onto the counter. Finished, he turned to her, his eyes narrowing and then widening slightly as his gaze moved over her, from her feet, which were covered by a pair of pink wool socks, to her hair, which had dried, but had not yet been brushed. They dwelt longest on her hips, snugly encased—too snugly, in fact—in the faded jeans. And then they moved up to her breasts.

Gioia could have sunk through the floor. She didn't dare look down, knowing precisely what she would see. The soft, thin cotton shirt she'd put on because it was old and comfortable would do little to disguise what was happening to her. Her whole body was remembering his touch. No matter what her head said, her body knew where it belonged.

Thad turned abruptly away to stare out through a window into the darkness beyond. "I grew up in half a dozen towns in the state of Virginia, managed to snag a football scholarship, spent a couple of years at William and Mary, then joined the police force. Later on I settled more or less permanently in Raleigh. Are we through in the kitchen?"

Far from satisfied, Gioia allowed herself to be led into the living room. She still had several dozen questions that needed answering, but she couldn't bring herself to voice the ones that loomed largest.

Without thinking, she took her usual place on the sofa, and Thad sat down beside her. He slipped his arm around her shoulders and drew her close to his side, and she tried to fight the swift need that rose inside her. "Is this the 'talking' you wanted to do?" She had tried to inject her voice with a note of concern, but it didn't quite come off.

"I've been aching for this all day." Thad leaned closer. Gioia stiffened. She saw it happening, and was totally helpless to prevent it.

That first kiss was as soft as the brush of a humming-bird's wing. He touched first her upper lip, then her lower lip—first one corner, then the other. And then he lifted his head and smiled down at her, a lazy, sleepy smile that sizzled its way down to her dominant index toes.

Like a sunflower seeking the light, she lifted her face the few inches it took to find his lips again. Laughing softly, he kissed the tip of her nose. She was trembling all over with need by the time he drew her across his lap.

This time when their lips met, there was nothing teasing, or even faintly apologetic about his kiss. His mouth twisted fiercely against hers, touching off fires, arousing hungers that had her hands digging into his back, stroking his sides, burrowing under his scratchy wool sweater. His tongue began a slow, seductive mating dance, and she lost all semblance of control.

God, how she wanted him! She'd thought—

But she'd been wrong. Because there was no mistaking the fact that he wanted her every bit as much as she wanted him.

"I'm so glad," she whispered aeons later when he lifted his head. He looked feverish, but then so must she. With her heart racing a mile a minute, her temperature was probably well into the danger zone. "Thad, why didn't you call? Or at least leave me a note?"

"Shhh," he whispered. His eyes were like some dark alien metal. His jaw suddenly seemed more aggressive, and even the cut of his cheekbones seemed sharper. And his lips! Still damp and swollen from her kisses, they were reaching for hers even now.

She tasted coffee and spice, and the essence of aroused male. It was intoxicating beyond belief. Thad somehow managed to arrange things so that she was practically lying on top of him, but it wasn't enough. She wanted to be closer still. She wanted his strength, his passion—even his stubbornness. All the things he was, she wanted, but most of all, she wanted canvas pants outlawed, retroactively!

His hands had tugged her shirt free of her jeans and were stroking her back. Her breasts ached for their touch. Callused, hard, his fingers were incredibly gentle. How was it possible for a man to be so hard and so tender at the same time?

And why didn't he take her to bed? What was he waiting for?

Thad shifted to allow his hands more freedom, and Gioia watched, frustrated, but beyond resisting as he lifted her shirt over her head and gazed at her breasts for what seemed a lifetime.

Instinctively she pressed herself against him. No matter what he had said last night, she was as flat as two fried eggs. Except for the obvious signs of her arousal. "Don't look at me," she pleaded.

"I can no more help looking at you than I can help touching you... wanting you. Needing you." His voice registered on her spine like the bass notes of a pipe organ.

He shifted once more until his face was against her breast. When once again she felt the hot, sweet torture of his tongue caressing her nipple, she pressed her head back against the cushion and closed her eyes. She was dying. That was all there was to it.

"Thad, please," she gasped when she could stand it no longer. "Can't we? That is, don't you want to... want me?"

He lifted his head, and she saw the beginning and end to all her dreams written there. "I've never wanted anything more in my life, sweet Joy. The trouble is, I've got no business wanting you when I can't offer you anything more than—" He shrugged, and even before he moved away, she felt the distance grow between them. It was as cold as Siberia.

"Yes, well, I guess that's plain enough." Was that her voice? It didn't sound like hers. "And you're right, you know. Except for—that is, in all the really important ways, we hardly even know each other. I don't know what I was thinking about to—"

He interrupted her. "Bull! You know more about me than any woman has in a long time."

With a forced brightness that nearly killed her, she shook her head. "I doubt that. And, anyway, we don't have a single thing in common. Do we?"

Thad felt as if he'd just kicked her. He hadn't meant to hurt her. God, that was the last thing he wanted! Every vestige of color had fled from her face, leaving her soft red lips and her dark blue eyes—eyes that were glittering too brightly—standing out in stark relief. She was the most beautiful thing he had ever seen at that moment—even with the red patch on her throat where his stubble had scraped her fragile skin.

Reaching out, he touched the place on her neck. Damn it, she was just so vulnerable! "I'm sorry. I'm too rough and you're so lovely. God, Joy, what am I going to do about you?"

"You could make love to me." Her voice was barely audible. "I'm not asking for any more than that—any more than you feel like giving. Honestly, I'm not, Thad."

He groaned. She had all the survival instincts of a butterfly! How could he take what she offered and then walk away? God knows who he was trying to protect—maybe he needed rescuing as much as she did!

"Honey, it would never work. You know it, I know it, so why not cut our losses? Besides, we're apt to have company any minute now, and I'm muddy. I need a shave and a shower. I'd hate to offend your tender sensibilities."

"Oh, by all means, let's not offend my tender sensibilities." She even managed a respectable grin. She'd survive this if it killed her. And it probably would. Striving for a nonincendiary topic, she said, "I wonder when T.J. and Angie will be back."

"Pretty soon now probably. So before they get here, maybe we'd better get a few things straight."

Drawing her feet up on the sofa, Gioia clutched her toes and was shocked to discover they were as cold as ice. "That darn furnace. I'm going to have to get the man out here again. Oh, by the way," she said brightly, needing to fill every moment with sound to prevent herself from thinking. "Did I tell you I have another refinishing job lined up after I finish the Timberlake place? It's an old hunt club near Waterlily. That's this little place right on the—"

"I know where it is."

"Inland waterway," she finished. And then she ran out of steam. Was this really the same man who had held her and made love to her as if he would never get enough of her? Or had she dreamed all that?

She must have dreamed it. Those varnish fumes again... "Look, maybe you'd better go," she said gruffly. Suddenly getting up, she stalked across the room and yanked an inoffensive leaf off her favorite prayer plant. "It's getting late, and I have a lot to do, and—"

Thad came up to stand behind her. Cupping her shoulders, he held fast when she tried to pull away. "Stop it, Gioia!"

"Stop what? I'm not doing anything, am I? Neither one of us is, thanks to your better judgment. I really appreciate your concern, Thad. I can't tell you how much. I mean, I get these wild ideas sometimes. Did I tell you about the reckless strain that runs through my family? Remind me to tell you about Granny G. and her sweet potato brandy sometime. Anyway, before I know it, I'm in trouble up to my neck, and—" Her eyes were glinting with unshed tears. Acute embarrassment always affected her this way. "Well, at least one of us has a sense of self-preservation. Thank goodness for that!''

Talk about reckless! And she'd always prided herself on being the sensible one in the family. So what did she do? Go and fall in love with a man who didn't love her back, and to make matters worse, she was handling the whole thing without a shred of dignity.

Thad was watching her like a sentry dog guarding its territory. Or rather, like a dog guarding a bone he didn't even want.

"I said we needed to talk and I meant it," he told her. "One thing you need to know is that I was married once. It was a bad marriage. Evidently neither one of us knew enough or cared enough to make it work. I don't make the same mistake twice, Gioia."

Eyes blazing, she spun around to face him. "Who the hell asked you?"

Ignoring her interruption, he said, "I'm not sure how long I'll be here. Not much longer probably. And as much as I want to sleep with you again—hell, to move in with you, for that matter—I know better. I don't think you'd handle it particularly well. I know I wouldn't, either. The trouble is, I like you too much, Gioia. Wanting is easy. If that's all there was, then I wouldn't be saying this. I'd be right back in your bed, doing my damnedest to make you think I was the greatest lover since Valentino."

Gioia's eyes were completely dry now. They burned with an intensity that she hoped he'd feel right through to his miserable cowardly soul! Because that's what he was—a coward! If she, with her lousy track record, could take a chance, then why couldn't he? What was so rare about a broken marriage? Most of her friends were on the second go-around. A few on the third.

She crossed her arms and stared him in the eyes, grateful, for once, for all five feet ten inches of height that she possessed. "Is that it?"

Thad blinked once. He wanted to say something else, but then he changed his mind. "I'll just get my coat," he muttered. "Tell T.J . . . Nothing."

His hand was on the doorknob when he turned on her, his dark eyebrows lowering like thunderclouds. "One more thing before I leave—I don't want you anywhere near that damn boat yard. Is that clear? This guy Smith—the one you were cozying up to this afternoon—he's one of the slickest operators in the business. He'd steal the *QE II* if he could find a buyer for it, and he's not about to let anyone get in his way."

"I haven't the slightest idea what you're talking about." Gioia took great pleasure in elevating her head until she could look down her nose. It wasn't near enough, but it helped.

"You know what I'm talking about, all right. In case your little visit included a tour of the facilities, with maybe a drink aboard the *Belle Star*—or the *Starfish*, or whatever the hell he's calling her now—you'd better know that the last two guys he entertained on board ended up dead! He might seem harmless on the surface, but he's a killer, Gioia. And if I see your car even slow down when you drive past that place, you're going to find out what protective custody's all about!"

He glared at her.

She glared back. She was so hurt, so furious, that she could barely bring herself to speak. "Oh, and I suppose the big macho detective plans to leap out from behind a bush and snap the cuffs on him before he knows what hit him, right? Make the world a safer place for mankind, right? Big hero!"

"You got a problem with that?"

His chin jutted toward her, and hers jutted back. "In that case I hope you have some good backup, someone with a few more brains than you've got. Like the Keystone Cops!"

Thad flung open the door and vaulted off the front porch, taking the three steps in a single leap. Gioia stared after him. Reaction had set in and she was shaking all over. Thank the Lord she'd had better sense than to get in any deeper than she already was!

Thad made three jabs with the ignition key before he hit the slot. He was so damn mad he was shaking! Who did she think she was, going on as if he were some slob who couldn't even tie his own shoes! Maybe he was no cardboard hero, but he got the job done!

Hell, the sooner he got it done, the better. He had to get away from here!

Ten

It rained for the next two days, a hard, cold December rain that was a perfect reflection of Gioia's mood. Thad didn't call, but then she hadn't really expected him to. What was there to say?

Even with the Christmas rush at the shop, T.J. managed to drop by twice. Angie met him for lunch both days, and they seemed to spend every possible moment together. Gioia was never awake when he brought her home at night, and by the time Angie woke the next morning, Gioia was already gone, which meant that Gioia was spared both a rehash of the old affair and a blow-by-blow of the new one.

In either case, she wouldn't have been a sympathetic listener.

The rain had postponed her trip to the fabric shop with

JoElla the first day, but on the second day, with no relief in sight, the two women decided to get it over with.

"I've got to get started if I'm going to get these things done in a week and a half," JoElla said.

"I thought you said a week."

"That was without the extras. He wants the name on every single cushion, like he was afraid somebody might forget whose boat they were sitting on or something. These fancy yachty people are the darnedest ones for showing off. Still, I reckon I shouldn't complain—they sure put me in the way of a lot of business."

Something stirred in Gioia's mind. She tried to bring it into focus, but with the problem of trying to make do with worn windshield wipers and a sluggish defroster, not to mention JoElla's chatter, it slipped away before she could latch on to it.

The shop was largely deserted. Any shoppers desperate enough to venture out on such a miserable morning were doing their Christmas shopping at the mall. JoElla, a boot on one foot and a shearling-lined slipper on the other, homed in on the upholstery section.

"What color?" asked Gioia. She had no real personal interest in fabric at the moment, but she always enjoyed the variety of color, pattern and weave. "Oh, look at this! Wouldn't I love to do a chair in this stuff. It would look elegant with a touch of polished cherry. One of these days..."

"If that's not just like a man," JoElla wailed. "Blue, he said! Like an idiot, I didn't even think to ask what shade of blue. This is just what he needs in a fabric. It's water repellent, stain repellent, and it looks as rich as cream.

Only does he want it in this turquoisey blue color, or the navy, or that rich cobalt?''

"Are you asking me?" Gioia wandered over to frown at the choices.

"At least you've seen the inside of the cabin, which is more than I have. Does he have any other colors in there? Or maybe he's planning to change those, too."

"There's carpet. I think it's a sort of blue-green tweed, but I wasn't paying all that much attention. The woodwork is gorgeous. I was mainly interested in that." She bit her lip as once again something tugged at her mind.

"What shade is the blue in the tweed? Which do you think would look best?"

Bingo! That green cushion—the *Belle Star*'s cushion. Thad had said that the stolen yacht he was trying to locate had originally been named the *Belle Star*. T.J. had mentioned when he was waiting for Angie to finish getting dressed the other night that Thad would probably be leaving pretty soon, as he was about to wind up the case he'd been working on.

"You mean the yacht thing?" she'd asked, trying to sound as if she were only casually interested—as if she hadn't cried until her tear ducts had threatened to go on strike.

"Yeah, that's the one. He's found out where she's been hiding, but he's having a hard time getting on board her."

"But why can't he just call the police and tell them where she is?"

"For one thing, he needs proof that she's the one that was stolen, and he can't get it without finding some way to board her. Only this guy Smith got a look at him twice, once in Georgia and once in South Carolina. If he sees him here, too, he's going to wonder."

Gioia had suddenly felt as if all the doors and windows in the house had suddenly been thrown open to the cold, damp night air. "Would he... I mean, is it really that dangerous?"

"You better believe it. It escapes me completely why a man with a brain as good as Thad's wants to mess around with people like that. I can think of a lot more interesting things to do with my life than getting my face pushed in and a few bones relocated."

Before she'd been able to find out more, Angie had come in, and they'd left in a breathless flurry of perfume and cologne.

"Listen," she said now to JoElla. "Why don't I do this?" She proceeded to outline her plan, and the two women stopped for pizzas before heading back to Riverton. "I've got the samples and I'll stop by the fabric place on the way home this evening and get whichever Mr. Smith decides on. Write down the yardage and any extras you'll be needing."

She wouldn't accept any more free pecans as thanks, because this next trip out to the boat yard was strictly her own business. She only hoped the cushion would still be there.

It was really so simple, Gioia thought later as she recrossed the bridge for the third time that day. If Thad had bothered to explain it all before he'd gotten her in such a state that she didn't know whether she was coming or going, she'd have remembered to tell him about the cushion. It might not be proof, but it was a whole lot better than anything he'd been able to find on his own, according to T.J.

But then if she'd told him, and he'd decided to go after the cushion alone, and Smith had caught him in the act...

Oh, no. It was much better this way. Safer for all concerned. No matter how surly old Yellow Shoes was, he wanted his cushions covered. She was beginning to understand why. But he'd have no reason to be suspicious of the woman who was, as far as he knew, working with the upholsterer on the job. I mean, she had samples, didn't she? And he wanted the job done right, didn't he? So what was more logical than that she make another trip out there and match the three shades of blue with his carpet to see which one went best?

Elmo Pritchard was there, along with a man who had to be his brother, if family resemblance was anything to go by. They were up to their elbows in a big chunk of greasy metal, tapping, grunting and cursing.

Seeing her, Elmo grinned shyly. The other man's smile was almost identical. He carefully wiped a wrench off, put it aside, then extended a hand that was black with grease.

Clutching her shoulder bag, Gioia smiled, touched his fingertips and stepped back quickly. She'd brought along her largest bag, stuffed with newspaper and topped off with the fabric swatches. "I was looking for Mr. Smith. Is he here?"

"Gone to the dentist. Borrowed my pickup. Reckon he'll be needing something to cheer him up when he gets back. So if you wanna wait, there's a bench over yonder." He gestured to an automobile seat perched on a base of concrete blocks. "You can watch us work."

"Oh, well, I—Do you happen to know when he'll be back?"

"No telling. If I was him, I'd go by the liquor store first and get me a big dose of painkiller. I expect he's gonna need it."

Gioia couldn't believe her good luck. Unless he'd locked everything up before leaving... "Oh, gee, well, you see, I really didn't need to see Mr. Smith so much as his carpet. In the main cabin. I'm doing some decorating for him, you know..." She waved the samples. "But I have to get back to my office, and I don't know when I'll get out this way again."

"Well, I reckon you could take a look at his rug, if that's all you need." The mechanic pointed at the row of boats with a grease-stained finger. "She's the last one in line, but I reckon you know where she is if you're doing her up for him."

What a streak of luck! If he'd locked the front door, then she'd find herself a hole or a window or a ventilator to slither through, because this was too great an opportunity to waste.

Her worries had been premature; the cabin was unlocked. It was also practically dark, thanks to the gloomy weather, and she hadn't the faintest idea of where to look for a light switch. If the cushion was still where she'd last seen it, she wouldn't need a light. She could grab it, stuff it into her shoulder bag instead of the crumpled newspaper, cover it with the swatches and get out before Smith ever knew she'd been there.

Except that it would have been nice to see the carpet so that she could tell JoElla which fabric would look best.

On the heels of that thought came another one: JoElla wouldn't be doing any cushions once Thad had taken Smith into custody, or whatever it was he planned to do with him. Which means she'd be out of the commission she'd counted on, one she really needed.

Oh, well, Gioia thought resignedly as she knelt in front of the locker and leaned down to reach behind it—she'd been planning on having that wing chair redone, anyway. This would be a good time to do it. What was more, she knew just the fabric she could use.

Feeling around in the narrow space, she muttered under her breath and pressed her shoulder against the corner, trying to extend her reach. It was no use. The cushion just wasn't there!

Oh, swell. So now what did she do? It couldn't have fallen out, and it was unlikely that it had gotten wedged any deeper, because the locker was only about three feet wide by two feet high. There was simply nowhere else it could go.

Thad pulled the Ford recklessly off the road and felt the right front tire sink into a morass of mud. He switched off the engine and was out and running before it quit turning over. Damn that woman. She didn't have enough brains to come in out of the rain! Pure contrariness, that's all it was! He'd told her not to come back, and she just had to show him!

Well, she'd shown him, all right! The minute he'd seen that monster car of hers, he'd blown a gasket. He'd murder the bearded bastard. If he had harmed a hair on her head, he was dead meat!

Before he reached the door, Thad made himself calm down. The gun he'd taken from its special place in his car was cold comfort as he opened the door a crack and peered inside.

Quiet. But not too quiet. Two men, the two he recognized as being the owners, were overhauling an engine in the near left-hand corner. To the right was a row of seven or eight boats. The first few had been hoisted up on chocks for extensive repairs, from the look of them. The last three, in the part of the shed built out over the water, were sailboats, the open roof at that end accommodating their masts. The whole east side of the metal building was open, sheltered somewhat from the weather by an assortment of ragged tarpaulins.

There was no sign of Gioia. She was evidently already aboard the ketch. God knows what had possessed her to do something so foolhardy—and after he'd warned her! All he could conclude was that she knew this guy better than she'd let on.

And that was what hurt. Damn, but it hurt!

"Hey, you looking for somebody, buster?"

Thad jerked his head around, all his senses alert. "Yeah, uh, did you see a woman come this way? About so tall, black hair? Drives a big yellow Lincoln?"

"You mean that decorator lady?"

That decorator lady. Okay, he could go along with that. "Yeah, that's the one. She still here? I missed her. I was supposed to come with her."

The mechanic shrugged his heavy, flannel-clad shoulders, as if to say it was no skin off his nose. "Last one on the end. How many of you guys does it take to look at a carpet, anyway?"

Look at a carpet? What the hell did that mean? "Oh, well, you know how it is." He tried for a knowing smile, but with his gut twisted painfully around his backbone and every old injury he'd ever received aching like the devil thanks to the rain, it probably didn't go over too well.

"Measurements, huh? Figgers. Wife measured a table leg that got broke so I could turn her a new one. Told me it come out thirty-two inches and a bunch o' them little doojiggers."

Thad was halfway down the row of boats already, trying hard to keep from breaking into a run. His right arm was flexed to bring his hand within inches of his gun. "Doojiggers, huh? Yeah, that's why they sent me along," he called over his shoulder. "Smith here?"

That was when he got the first indication that there was a God in heaven after all.

"Nah, like I told the lady, he had him this toothache. Been nursing it all week. I lent him my truck and sent him off to ol' Doc Funderburk 'bout an hour ago."

By now Thad was all the way at the end of the row. He took only half a moment to gaze with satisfaction at the *Belle Star*, alias *Starfish*. And now known as *Sea Fever*, he noted with a grim look as he leaped lightly aboard and crossed the scrupulously maintained deck.

On her knees, Gioia froze. She scrambled to pull the swatches out of her bag and spread them on the floor. Deck. Whatever! "Oh, my, this isn't going to work," she said aloud, hoping Smith would be too far gone on painkillers to notice the tremor in her voice, or the fact that she was squeaking like a terrified mouse—which she was.

"You might try turning on a light."

Already on her knees, she could only collapse onto her elbows and bury her face in her arms. Dear God, she'd thought it was all over for sure!

"And you might try announcing your presence instead of sneaking up on a body and scaring her to death!"

"You want to know about *scared*? Try being gagged and trussed up with about fifty feet of duct tape and crammed into an airtight locker! Try going for a moonlight sail and being asked to walk home! Try—'' He broke off, unable to go on. The sight of her long, elegant body sprawled at his feet, her face buried under a cloud of hair and her shapely behind jutting up into the air like twin volcanic islands made him feel like crying. Or cursing. But it was those feet of hers, the right one curled over the left one, that finished him off.

Two steps and he was beside her. He was just bending over to lift her up when she looked up at him, her face a pale oval in the gray light that spilled in through the portholes.

''You're standing on my swatch,'' she snapped.

''I'm standing on your *what*?''

''Swatch! Swatch!'' Grabbing the one that wasn't anchored by a large booted foot, she stood up and shook it under his nose. ''This thing, you idiot! What are you doing here, anyway? Don't you have a grain of sense? That man will be back here any minute now, and he's not going to be real happy to find you here. You said yourself that he's dangerous.''

''So that's why you came tearing out here, right? You're attracted to danger?''

They were standing toe to toe, and no matter how cleverly the cabin had been designed to make the most of the limited space, there wasn't enough room. Gioia felt as if her lungs were starved for air, and from the look on his face, Thad wasn't in much better shape.

''I really think you'd better leave before Smith gets back. Let me handle this.'' She was still struggling for control of her voice.

''Would you mind telling me just what it is you're planning on *handling* And *why*?''

She stepped back, and he stepped forward, crowding her against the curving bulkhead. "You don't have to get pushy," she began when he grabbed her by the arms and shook her until her hair was dancing like a willow in a March wind.

"Pushy! Do you have any idea just how pushy I'd *like* to get? I'd like to push you out of here on your obstinate rear end, and then push you down in a chair and sit on you until you give me your word that you'll never—*ever*—pull a crazy stunt like this again! Don't you know you could have gotten yourself *killed*? Why the hell did you think I warned you away from here?"

And then his voice broke, and she was in his arms, and he was still swearing, but somehow it sounded different. Gioia didn't know just how she knew; she only knew it was different.

"I only wanted to find the cushion so you'd have your blasted proof and...and you wouldn't get your face pushed in or your b-bones relocated, or whatever. It's dangerous! T.J. said if that man ever caught you messing around, he'd probably recognize you. And you said yourself that he's a...a k-killer."

"What cushion? No, don't tell me. First I'm going to get you out of here, and then you can tell me everything. And damn it, stop crying, will you? You'll have me doing it!"

"I'm not crying," Gioia protested automatically as she let herself be led outside. "My eyes just happen to be sensitive. They water a lot."

"Yeah, sure," he said, his voice rough-edged as he hurried her past where the two Pritchard brothers were engrossed in their operation.

Flattening himself against the wall, Thad eased the door open and slipped outside. He looked around carefully, and only then did he allow her to join him. "Let's take your car," he growled. "Mine's stuck in the mud again."

By the time they defrosted the windshield enough to see out, Gioia was having second thoughts. She was driving, while Thad was watching the road, suspicious of every vehicle they passed.

Blackened cypresses dripped rain and Spanish moss along the riverfront as they drove the few miles back to Riverton. "Thad, we're really missing a great opportunity. I mean, with Smith gone we could find the cushion I saw with *Belle Star* on it. That should give you the proof you need and you could turn the whole thing over to the police, and—"

"Whoa! Where did you get this 'we' stuff? There's no 'us' about it. No royal 'we.' *You* are going home, and *I* am going to go about my business with no more outside interference. Is that clear?"

A fifty-pound weight settled slowly onto her heart. She blinked her eyes, which had suddenly gotten sensitive again. "Well, of course I know that," she said with quiet dignity. "I never thought there was a-an 'us.'"

No, of course you didn't, you witless wonder, that's why you lie awake for hours visualizing all those stubborn, tough little boys and little girls with their clear hazel eyes and streaky dark blond hair.

They drove the rest of the way in silence. The rain showed signs of ending, but that couldn't rescue her spirits. At this point she doubted she'd ever smile again.

"Almost there," she said. "Shall I call you a taxi?"

"Thanks, but I plan to borrow your car. That way I can be sure you stay put."

"You're crazy if you think I'm going to let you—"

"But first," Thad said, completely ignoring her protests. "I need to look at your phone book. Have you got anything sweet I could eat on the road? That last burst of adrenaline just about did me in."

Gioia stalked off ahead of him, telling herself she hoped he slipped on her wet porch steps and broke his thick, stubborn neck. "I suppose next you'll be wanting coffee to go? How about an order of french fries?"

"Sorry. I'm in too big a hurry. But it wouldn't hurt you to get something hot inside you. This rain soaks right through to the bone."

Ten minutes later Thad pulled into the parking lot and cruised the row of vehicles parked there. There were four pickup trucks, two of them red, but he spotted Pritchard's right away. It was the one with the rifle rack and the heavy-duty trailer hitch.

His luck was holding. He'd counted on the dentist's not being able to work in an emergency patient right away. With any luck the guy would need root canals done on every tooth in his head, which would give him just about enough time to get the proof he needed. And if he could lay hands on the monogrammed cushion Gioia had been looking for, that would be the clincher.

After that, it would be all over but the shouting. He could wind the whole thing up and get on with something a little more important.

Pulling into a slot three spaces down, Thad licked cake frosting off his fingers and got out, glancing quickly in both directions first.

Something a *lot* more important, he told himself, a slow smile spreading across his face as he knelt to unscrew the valve cap on the left rear tire.

* * *

Gioia puttered. From puttering she sank to fidgeting. Every dish in the house was washed, the whole house was clean, and for once, she wasn't in the mood to listen to music or to read. She turned on the TV, then turned it off again. The last thing she needed to watch was someone else's soap opera. Her own was more than enough.

Angie was out with T.J. again. They'd known each other for what, three days? Four? And already they were practically inseparable. Something had to be done about these Creed men. The surgeon general needed to put out a proclamation.

She'd felt awful when she'd had to call JoElla and tell her about the cushions. Of course, the real owner might want them redone, since Smith had evidently destroyed his pretty green covers. More likely, he'd just want to get clean out of this area and forget about the whole miserable business.

Gioia could sympathize with that. If she weren't saddled with this house, she wouldn't mind cutting her losses and moving on herself. To someplace new, someplace that wouldn't remind her constantly of a certain tough, rough, unhandsome man who didn't have time or room in his life for someone like her.

"Hockey pucks," she muttered, yanking another leaf off her lemon balm geranium. The poor thing was already in shock. She felt like a murderer, but she had to take out her frustration on something, and she didn't happen to have a punching bag.

When she heard her car returning, she was laboriously prying the upholstery tacks off the arms of her wing chair. At least he'd brought the car back. Straddling a cabriole leg, she jimmied the screwdriver under another tack and

lifted enough to get the claw hammer under the head, deliberately letting him cool his heels before she got up to
unlock the door.

Taking her time, she opened it only halfway. "Thanks
for returning my car," she said stiffly. She didn't invite him
inside, but Thad had never been one to stand on cere-
mony.

"Don't you even want to know how it went?"

"It's none of my business. I'm sure I don't even know
what you're—"

"Okay, so we'll play it your way." With a look that
would have sent any sane person scrambling for cover, he
scooped her up in his arms, slung her over his shoulder and
headed for the bedroom.

"Thaddeus, I'm warning you. Put me down this minute, or you'll be walking on crutches for the next ten
years!" She sounded more breathless than furious, which
made matters worse, if possible. The breathlessness occurred only because she was hanging head down in what
had to be the most uncomfortable, undignified position
known to man. "Thad, I'm warning you!" She ham-
mered on his rear end, which happened to be in perfect
range of her fists.

Ignoring her outrage, Thad proceeded to dump her onto
the bed like a sack of corn. While she caught her breath,
he stood grinning down at her like some victorious war-
lord gloating over his share of the spoils.

"You know you'll pay dearly for this for the rest of your
natural-born days," she promised, her eyebrows drawn
down threateningly.

"Yep."

The man was totally despicable and totally irresistible.
It was a horrid combination! "Am I to gather from all this

that everything worked out and you're now the big hero?'' Sarcasm coated each word like a sugary frosting.

''Yep.''

He was grinning that wicked grin of his, and the more he did it, the more it got under her skin, until suddenly it was just too much. All the tension of the past few hours—of the past few days, in fact—swelled up and spilled over, and she rolled over onto her stomach and buried her face in the pillow, shoulders shaking with laughter. She simply wasn't cut out for high tragedy. Never had been.

Thad came down beside her, tilting the mattress so that she rolled against his hips. His hand warm on her neck, he brushed her hair away so that he could peer at her face. ''Hey, don't cry. I'll leave. I only thought you might want to know that I found your cushion. It was buried under that pile of junk out behind the shed. He was probably planning to burn it once the rain stopped. Besides that, I located two HINs. Smith's in custody now, and so damn miserable with a dry socket that he doesn't even—''

''A dry what?''

''Uh, something about a wisdom tooth. Don't ask me. I'm no dentist. Anyway, Summerfield's on his way up from Florida, and the cops are questioning Elmo and Claremont, but I'm pretty satisfied they didn't know what was going on. So my part's done, and now I can—''

''You don't have to say any more. I understand.'' She gave one last shuddering sob—of laughter. Her eyes always watered when she laughed. He was leaving, damn his insensitive hide, and she tried to tell herself she didn't care, that she'd be better off without him. ''Sorry I got in your way. I was only trying to help.''

''I know you were. It's just that, well, damn it, honey, I lost five years off my life when I found out you were wad-ing in right up to your pretty little neck in spite of everything I told you about that guy. Don't you have a grain of common sense?''

With one last sniffle, Gioia rolled back over and stared up at him through the tangle of her hair. Her eyes met his, and she felt herself sinking fathoms deep. "I always thought I did. Lately I've had cause to wonder."

"Yeah, well take my word for it, you don't. Women like you need a keeper, and—"

At that, she sat bolt upright, patches of color suddenly blooming in her cheeks. "Oh, now w-wait a minute, buster! Don't you accuse me of—"

"I'm applying for the job."

"Needing a keeper, because for twenty-seven years, I've—*What did you say?*"

"I said, I'm asking you to marry me. You got a problem with that?"

Gioia crossed her legs, propped her elbows on her thighs and stared at him until a raw flush began to creep up over his leathery cheeks. "Why?" she said finally.

Thad shrugged. He had stood up again, and now his hands were rammed into his pockets. He had that bulldoggish look that had first endeared him to her. "Why? Well, for all the usual reasons, I reckon. Why not?"

"You want reasons why not? Hold up your fingers. I don't have enough to even begin to count! There's the fact that you're going back to Raleigh and I'm staying here, for starters."

"You wouldn't have to stay here. I'd move my offices here, but I have to tell you, there are advantages to being located in a city, especially the capital. Besides, I know the guys on the force there, and that can come in handy."

"There's the fact that we don't have a single thing in common—at least not all that much."

One hand had emerged from his pocket, and he was absently stroking her left knee. "Yeah. Makes things kind of interesting, doesn't it? One thing for sure, we won't get bored."

Gioia shifted her left leg, and his hand fell away. A bit unevenly she said, "Well, but what about, uh..."

"What I said about not wanting to get married again?"

She nodded silently, not trusting herself to speak. Thad sat down beside her, and this time he took her hand, and there was no way she could pull away. Even if she'd wanted to.

"Getting married then was a pretty stupid thing to do, only I didn't see it that way at the time. I only knew I wanted to prove something to my dad, and I ended up proving I was just as big a loser as he was."

"You're *not* a loser. You could *never* be a loser," she said fervently, leaning close so that the top of her head almost brushed the top of his, with only her crossed legs holding them apart.

"Yeah, well...at least I learn from my mistakes. Jackie and I were too young, and we married for the wrong reasons. I didn't blame her when she left me. Hell, what woman in her right mind wants to be tied to a jerk who can't even put on his own pants? For all she knew, I'd never have been able to walk, much less, uh, anything else."

"I'd think a woman would want to stick by her man even more under those circumstances."

"To hell with that!" he said immediately. "You think I want pity from a woman?"

Gioia's lips twitched, but she was careful not to allow him to see it. "You might want it, but you probably wouldn't get it. You're hardly the type to elicit any such tender emotion."

"Is that right? Is that why you nearly got your head broken, not to mention a few other portions of your anatomy, trying to keep me out of trouble?"

Happiness bubbled up and overflowed all over her face. "That was only because I owed you for fixing my flat, remember?"

"Yeah, well, now you owe me for—hold on, I'll think of something in a minute. So what do you say? Are you going to marry me?"

"Is that the best you can do?"

"What, you want romance? I can handle that. You just wait right here. Don't move a muscle. No, on second thought, get into something soft and pretty. I'll show you romance!"

Gioia couldn't stop smiling. On the inside and the outside. Her ears were smiling, her stomach, too. Even her toes were smiling, if that was possible.

And at the moment it seemed that anything was.

Thank goodness she had a few things stored here, so there was something appropriate for her to slip into.

Unfortunately her attire hadn't been designed for warmth, and the bedroom was still too cold for comfort.

She heard Thad go out and come in, and then she could hear him out in the kitchen. He was singing, his voice not half bad if one happened to like chocolate-covered gravel. And suddenly she did.

But then she heard another voice, this one coming over the stereo, and it was deep and soft and lazy; it licked at her spine and sent tremors down her limbs.

Thad appeared in the doorway holding up two wine-glasses and a bottle. "I don't guarantee this stuff, but T.J. buys it by the case. Drinks are on him tonight."

And then his eyes widened, and the bottle tilted dangerously. "Oh, geeze, sweetheart, I'm not sure I can get through this. Maybe you'd better cover up or something."

"What's the matter? Don't you like it? I thought men were supposed to like black lace."

He set the bottle and glasses on the bedside table, knocked over one of the glasses and caught it before it hit the floor. "Do you, uh, wear that kind of thing very often?"

"Not too often. I've had this one for several years, and I've never gotten around to wearing it. It's really not very practical, you know." *Eat your heart out, John Pirelli!*

"Damn right it's not. I'd hate to get a reading on my blood pressure about now." As if snapping himself out of a trance, he switched off the overhead light. The floor lamp nearest the bedroom door in the living room—the one with the pink shade—had been left on, and from her stereo on the bookshelf beside it, that voice was doing peculiar things to her insides.

"Okay, I have to admit, you've got romantic down to a fine art, but don't you have something to say?" she purred, accepting a glass of wine. She sipped, and T.J. rose one more notch in her estimation.

"Patience, honey, I'm getting there." Cautiously he sipped. And then he sipped again. "Not bad. Wouldn't stand up to a stiff Mexican dinner, but it's not all that bad."

He'd removed his bulky sweater, and Gioia gazed appreciatively at his well-developed torso, nicely delineated by the black wool knit shirt. He looked a lot warmer than she was at the moment, but that was improving rapidly.

"You like my music?" he asked, slipping off his shirt and boots and sliding onto the bed beside her.

"The way you like the wine," she teased. "Not bad." Actually, it was surprisingly good. The man could not only sing, he could sing in a way that ... Well, suffice it to say, it that was meant to be mood music, she was definitely getting in the mood! "Who is he?" she asked, trying her best to sound more relaxed than she felt.

"That's old Don. I want you to listen real careful to what he's saying, okay?"

"I'd much rather listen to you." She touched his eyebrow and let her fingertip trail down his temple and curl around his ears. He was right. His were twice as large as hers were, and she loved every tasty morsel of them.

As if to prove it, she leaned closer and took a small nibble. "Well?"

"You see, this song he's singing now," Thad went on as seriously as if he weren't visibly aroused to the point of danger. "It's all about this guy who can't come up with the right way to say things. So he tells the woman he loves to listen to the radio and let the songs tell her how much he loves her, how he wants her, how she's this big ache in his soul when he's not with her, and he doesn't think he can face living without her for another day, and he wants to spend the rest of his life and then some with her. Stuff like that."

Gioia thought her heart would burst. She wrapped her arms around his neck and nuzzled his throat, too overwrought to speak. How on earth had she been so lucky? What if they'd *missed* each other? Of all the men in the world, only this one had been created especially for her, and handsome or not, articulate or not, she wouldn't change a single thing about him.

"For a man who pretends to be so tough," she murmured as her hands began a slow, heated search of his hard, rugged body, "you're a real pushover, aren't you?"

"There's only one woman in the world who can get away with making a statement like that," Thad growled, bringing his lips down until they brushed against hers. "I think I'd better arrange to keep her under permanent surveillance, don't you?"

His kiss had her reeling like a drunken butterfly. Somehow she'd managed to lose her black lace nightgown, but she certainly wasn't suffering from the cold.

When she could speak again, she said, "You'd better keep her under *something*, anyway. I could offer a suggestion or two."

From the living room, Don Williams started in on another love song, but he had already lost his audience.

Epilogue

Honey, I'm home!"

"I'm out here," Gioia called back. She was just finishing the last coat on the inlaid walnut liquor cabinet. It had been a real find, but instead of taking it to the shop, which she'd named Gioia's Attic, and which was keeping her so busy she'd had to hire an assistant, she'd decided to bring it home. With the legs cut down and a few minor revisions inside, it was going to make a perfect place to store Thad's tapes and her albums out of the way of curious little fingers.

Brushing aside her braid, Thad leaned down and kissed the back of her neck. "Mmmm, Ivory soap and turpentine, my favorite perfume. You ought not to be crawling around like that in your delicate condition, sweetheart."

"Poo! Look who got me in this condition! And delicate's the last word I'd use to describe it. Angie invited us to go to Riverton for Thanksgiving." They had only been back three times in the five years since they'd been married, what with buying the house, getting the shop established, and going out to Oklahoma to the wedding of Thad's mother and all. "Is that okay with you?"

"Sure," Thad drawled, toying with his wife's braid, which he refused to allow her to cut off.

"What about your mother? Do you think she'd mind too much?"

"She'll be spending the holidays with her new husband's family. Anyhow, she probably won't get too possessive until after the baby comes. After that, though, watch out!"

"After that she can fight it out with Mama and Daddy. At least we won't have trouble finding baby-sitters. Angie sent pictures, by the way. They're on the mantel."

Thad wandered out, and Gioia gazed after him, her entire face glowing with a love that seemed to grow stronger each year they were together. Thad's concession to being a staid business man, owner of one of the most successful investigative agencies in the area, was to wear soft corduroy jackets that more or less matched his slacks, and to start out the day, at least, wearing a necktie.

"Hey, the old house is looking pretty good, isn't it?" he called from the living room. "I sort of miss the orange paint, though."

"Notice anything else?" Gioia levered herself awkwardly to her feet and strolled in to join her husband.

"You mean the fact that T.J.'s hairline's headed west?"

"I mean, the fact that Lucy looks more like Angie every day. You see the way T.J.'s beaming at her? It's a good thing she's going to have a little brother pretty soon, or she'd be one spoiled little girl."

"Yeah, I guess. You know T.J. He gains ten pounds every time Angie get pregnant."

"He's just a tiny bit portly. In a double-breasted suit it hardly shows."

"What he needs is a male maternity suit," Thad said with a chuckle. After a year and a half of office work, he was as lean and hard as ever. Gioia prided herself that she'd known all along which of the Creed men would wear best.

"Hey, lady, go put your feet up. Tonight I'm cooking, remember?"

"Mexican?" She nuzzled as close as she could get in the eighth month of pregnancy and pressed a kiss on the tiny scar on one side of his chin.

"Broiled bluefish with green chili sauce and shrimp tacos, okay?"

"Toss you for the dinner music. Heads we listen to Segovia, tails it's Dwight Yoakam."

Before she could move away, Thad caught her face between his hands, his eyes brimming with more love than a tough, nonromantic type would ever be able to express. "I'll be glad when we can risk a little more Don Williams, won't you? Cuddling's nice, but a man sort of misses other things after a while."

"After a while," Gioia promised, the photos falling unnoticed to the floor as Thad turned her in his arms and cradled her full breasts in his hands.

"After a while," he echoed, and the words held both hunger and an immense, soul-deep satisfaction.

*   *   *   *   *

A compelling novel of deadly revenge and passion
from bestselling international
romance author Penny Jordan

Eleven years had passed but the
terror of that night was something
Pepper Minesse would never
forget. Fueled by revenge against
the four men who had brutally
shattered her past, she set in
motion a deadly plan to destroy
their futures.

Available in February!

SILHOUETTE DESIRE™
presents
AUNT EUGENIA'S TREASURES
by CELESTE HAMILTON

Liz, Cassandra and Maggie are the honored recipients of Aunt Eugenia's heirloom jewels…but Eugenia knows the real prizes are the young women themselves. Read about Aunt Eugenia's quest to find them everlasting love. Each book shines on its own, but together, they're priceless!

Available in December:
THE DIAMOND'S SPARKLE (SD #537)

Altruistic Liz Patterson wants nothing to do with Nathan Hollister, but as the fast-lane PR man tells Liz, love is something he's willing to take *very* slowly.

Available in February:
RUBY FIRE (SD #549)

Impulsive Cassandra Martin returns from her travels… ready to rekindle the flame with the man she never forgot, Daniel O'Grady.

Available in April:
THE HIDDEN PEARL (SD #561)

Cautious Maggie O'Grady comes out of her shell…and glows in the precious warmth of love when brazen Jonah Pendleton moves in next door.

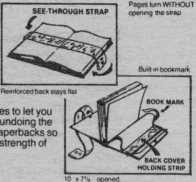

Silhouette Romances

Diana Palmer brings you an Award of Excellence title... and the first Silhouette Romance DIAMOND JUBILEE book.

ETHAN
by Diana Palmer

This month, Diana Palmer continues her bestselling LONG, TALL TEXANS series with *Ethan*—the story of a rugged rancher who refuses to get roped and tied by Arabella Craig, the one woman he can't resist.

 The Award of Excellence is given to one specially selected title per month. Spend January with *Ethan* #694... a special DIAMOND JUBILEE title... only in Silhouette Romance.

At long last, the books you've been waiting for
by one of America's top romance authors!

DIANA PALMER
DUETS

Ten years ago Diana Palmer published her very first
romances. Powerful and dramatic, these gripping tales
of love are everything you have come to expect from
Diana Palmer.

In March, some of these titles will be available again in
DIANA PALMER DUETS—a special three-book collection. Each book will have two wonderful stories plus an
introduction by the author. You won't want to miss them!

Book 1
SWEET ENEMY
LOVE ON TRIAL

Book 2
STORM OVER THE LAKE
TO LOVE AND CHERISH

Book 3
IF WINTER COMES
NOW AND FOREVER

Silhouette Books®